SNOW SOUNDS

Heather Williams

A KISMET™ Romance

METEOR PUBLISHING CORPORATION
Bensalem, Pennsylvania

KISMET™ is a trademark of Meteor Publishing Corporation

Copyright © 1991 Vella Munn
Cover Art Copyright © 1991 Alex Zwarenstein

All rights reserved.

No part of this book may be reproduced, stored in a retrieval system, or transmitted in any form, by any means, including mechanical, electronic, photocopying, recording or otherwise, without prior written permission of the publisher, Meteor Publishing Corporation, 3369 Progress Drive, Bensalem, PA 19020.

First Printing June 1991.

ISBN: 1-878702-47-5

All the characters in this book are fictitious. Any resemblance to actual persons, living or dead, is purely coincidental.

Printed in the United States of America

To my mother, who explored Mammoth Lakes with me. Thank you for your patience, your time, and most of all, the wonderful memories.

HEATHER WILLIAMS

There's a basic truth in the idea that you can't take the country out of the girl. Heather Williams grew up in logging camps, revitalized gold towns, and farming country. That, she believes, is why she writes about small town and wilderness experiences. When Heather's not writing, she's counting the days until her sons are out of college and paying their own bills so she and her husband can explore more of this country's back roads. Then she'll come home, look out at the Oregon forests, and write some more.

ONE

The mountain waited. It could be patient for the blanketing snows that turned Mammoth Lakes into a mecca for southern California skiers. For tens of thousands of years, the seasons had played their songs on rock and trees and water and earth. Ant-people scurried about its base, putting last winter behind them and preparing for the next. Those who toiled to control the mountain might not have ageless perspective, but the mountain did. Long after these intruders left, the songs and seasons would continue.

Although this wasn't her first time here, Melaine Landa couldn't imagine looking up at Mammoth without being touched by the mountain's power. Until a few seconds ago, she'd been filled with awe and peace, the sense that she'd come home.

But that was endless heartbeats ago. The builder of the almost-finished first-aid clinic she stood in had just said the one name she hoped she'd never hear again.

Tanner Harris.

Now there was only the name. And the memories.

Bert Edmonds pointed to the bank of windows facing Phantom's Escape. "The ski patrol's pretty excited about this project," he said. "Especially the communication system we'll have with the runs. When you've got ten thousand people coming through here on a weekend, there's got to be a way to keep tabs on them.''

Melaine turned. She no longer saw the great mass that would soon be transformed into a lacework of ski trails. She no longer cared about the challenge of the job she'd taken on as the clinic's resident nurse. "Tanner Harris," she managed "He's heading the ski patrol?"

"You know him?"

Melaine sidestepped the question. "How—long has he been here?"

"This'll be his third winter. Yeah. That's right. Used to run things for the patrol at Squaw Valley. He said it was time to tackle something different. He got that all right. Insane hours. One emergency after another. But there's good fishing, and Tanner likes to fish."

"I know." *Tanner was here. Why hadn't she faced that possibility?*

"You know Tanner likes to fish?"

Uneasy, Melaine addressed the question as best she could. "I mean . . . I worked here a couple of summers when I was in college. I know about Crowley Lake, Owens River. I took a cutthroat out of McCloud once that—" In the distance, a tram with one occupant slowly made its way to the top of Holiday. This time of year, only employees would be on the naked mountain. The person in the chair could be anyone. And it might be Tanner. Tanner, with a body conditioned by the elements, and words and emotions that had once touched her with proof that she was still alive.

"Then this isn't your first time here," Bert said. "I wondered."

"No." Melaine laced her fingers together, gripping tightly. "That's one of the reasons I wanted this job. I loved the area so much."

"It's changed a lot, hasn't it?"

Turning her back on the distant stranger in the chair

lift, Melaine focused on the smiling, weathered resort employee. "It's incredible. I can't believe the condominiums and lodges in the village. The shopping facilities. There are even fast-food restaurants."

"I know. Ain't it a mess." Bert laughed and moved closer to the window, taking Melaine's eyes, and thoughts, back to the mountain. "Actually," he went on, "if we have to have progress, I guess it doesn't look that bad. A few developers have kinda forgotten we're surrounded by wilderness, not L.A., but most of the places aren't hard on the eyes."

Melaine wanted to shake her head, press her hand against her eyes, anything that might make it easier to absorb the fact that this sheltered and isolated community high above the desert of central California had become Tanner's home. But she couldn't hide, and she couldn't escape reality. Unless she turned her back on this opportunity to rebuild her life, she'd have to face him. Weather his hate.

But not yet. Melaine ran her hand over a pine shelf, feeling strength. "I've been making lists of the supplies I'll need," she told Bert. "Lists and revised lists. There isn't going to be any trouble getting what I need, is there?"

"I wouldn't think so. You've got time to get this place stocked and under operation before the skiing season opens. And if you run low on supplies during the winter . . . There might be a few storms when we can't get anything out, but most of the time, nothing stops me and the rest of the pilots."

They'd left the front door open. The tender and yet penetrating scent of evergreens swirled around Melaine. A name had taken her apart a minute ago. Now the breeze helped her put the pieces back together. "Those storms? Has that ever caused a problem with reaching an injured skier?"

Bert shook his head. "Not likely. The ski patrol isn't

going to let anyone up the mountain if the weather's really bad. Big storm blows in and the lifts and trams stop operating. The patrol's always checking snow buildup, and, if necessary, they blast so there won't be an avalanche."

"Your ski patrol . . ." Melaine couldn't bring herself to mention the man carrying the ultimate responsibility. "It sounds as if they're prepared for everything."

"As prepared as anyone can be. Talk to Tanner. He'll tell you a lot more than I can."

Tanner.

For the next hour, Melaine followed Bert while he showed her around the clinic. She would have two examination rooms, storage space, and a small office which included the sophisticated communication system necessary to ensure the safety of skiers on both Mammoth and June Mountains.

"There isn't a thing I would change," Melaine told Bert as they were leaving. "Patients can easily be brought in here, and with the equipment I'll have, I'll be able to handle the majority of accidents and stabilize those I can't until we can get them to the hospital. You say there are five new patrol members . . . Tanner is going to be training?"

"He's already got that going." Bert started toward his Bronco. "Are you going to get in touch with him today? There's a lot the two of you have to work on."

No. Not today. Not until she could say his name without remembering their single, incredible night together.

Bert kept the conversation going during the drive to the lakeside A-frame Melaine had rented. He'd suggested she drop by his place for coffee, but she'd begged off, using as her excuse the boxes of belongings waiting to be unpacked. She promised Bert she'd call his wife later and then stepped inside the small, weathertight house with its airy combination living-dining-kitchen area and, above, the two loftlike bedrooms.

Although she'd only been in it long enough to drop off suitcases and boxes, Melaine already loved the unique house tucked into the trees around June Lake. Being hired for this position, being able to go back to the isolated village where she'd spent two marvelous summers, finding the kind of house she would have designed herself, knowing how free Amber would feel here—everything had felt somehow preordained.

Melaine stood next to the floor-to-ceiling window and drank in air so clean she cold taste its purity. From her place, she couldn't see the mountain or anyone who might be moving on it, but she imagined Tanner at the highest peak. He would stand in incredible isolation, touched by nothing except the wind. He'd look out at his world, seeing miles and miles of unspoiled beauty, thinking, not of the responsibilities that brought him here, but of the sense of peace that was part of solitude.

What would Tanner think when he learned that their paths had crossed? Would her name be an oath on his lips? Probably not. Three years was a long time. She wouldn't be more than a dim, unwanted memory to him.

Melaine Landa. Long limbs and a slight yet strong frame. Light-brown hair with hints of gold dancing in its depths. And her eyes—incredibly large, incredibly dark eyes. Eyes capable of swallowing a man.

Melaine. It was a name, only a name.

One he still carried inside him.

"Why didn't someone tell me the nurse was here? No. Never mind. It's all right. It sounds as if she had enough to do without my trying to hook up with her right away." Tanner held the walkie-talkie close to his mouth so he could be heard over the sound of a snowplow being tuned a hundred feet away. He'd put on his boots at 5 A.M. and hadn't taken time for lunch. Because he'd been in a hurry, he was going to have a bruise on his right shin from trying to shimmy around an overhang.

The lift he'd used earlier swung listlessly. There were a few vehicles in the parking lot, all of them belonging to employees, but except for the sweating, swearing mechanic hunched over the snowmobile, there weren't any other people around. As soon as the snows began to fall, the parking lot would pulse with skiers intent on jamming a winter's vacation into two or three days. Now, however, there was nothing to keep a woman's name from knifing its way into him.

Bert said something about having taken Melaine Landa to the clinic and being impressed by her professionalism. Tanner stared at his free hand, a hand that for a few unbelievable hours had known what a slim woman with fathomless eyes needed to bring her to life.

Damn it, he wouldn't be reminded of how much he'd given of himself during those hours. He would function as what he was, director of the National Ski Patrol for Mammoth and June mountains. With words that came automatically, Tanner asked Bert to bring him up to date on the new telephone wires that were to have been in place last week. Bert had received a promise from the telephone company to the effect that installation would be completed before Friday. "There's nothing written in blood, so I wouldn't bet the bank on this," Bert told him. "But they know we're running out of patience."

Tanner's hard laugh vibrated. "That's an understatement. When someone says they're going to do something, why can't they follow through?"

"I'm not the one to ask. Relax, will you? It'll get done."

"Eventually. Look, I'm not taking it out on you. All I'm asking for is a little honesty." Tanner was angry; he also knew he couldn't tell his friend the reason. "Damn it, they knew they weren't going to get to us when they said they would. Why people can't be up front—"

Why, indeed? Tanner asked himself hours later when the long day was over and he'd settled himself in his rustic cabin with its homemade wood furniture. Honesty was important to him, maybe the most important yardstick by which he judged himself and others.

He told the truth. He expected the same in return.

TWO

What do you hope to prove?

Tanner turned from the mocking question and went back to preparing for the evening's EMT training session. He'd met with the new patrol members night before last. Tonight the real work of assessing the building on their understanding of emergency medicine would begin. Until he'd been hit with the identity of the resident nurse, he'd simply assumed she would be part of the sessions.

Now that was the last thing he wanted.

Only, Melaine Landa had intruded on his life again. They would be working together, dealing with the practical aspects of setting up a new clinic, sharing the moments of high drama and urgency that came to Mammoth in the winter. No matter how he hated the prospect, he couldn't ignore it.

Tanner picked up the phone, thinking of nothing except his need to make Melaine understand how he felt. A moment later he hung up. He didn't know her number. But he did know how to get that necessary and unwanted information. Carol Edmonds answered after the fourth ring.

"You're lucky you caught me in," Carol said between quick breaths. "That blasted Star got loose again. It took a whole bucket of grain and a week's worth of patience to coax her back in. Now I've got to replace the two-by-four she kicked out. Dog meat! She's going to be dog meat."

"I keep telling you," Tanner said in continuation of a long-running mock argument between the two of them, "if you'd let me harness that nag to a gravel truck, I'd keep her so busy she wouldn't have the energy to act up."

"Don't tempt me. Bert isn't here. Is there something I can do?"

"You can give me a phone number. I need to get ahold of the nurse, Mrs. Landa."

"Mrs. Landa. Aren't we formal? Oh, wait a minute. You haven't met her, have you?"

Yes. I have. In another lifetime. Wondering at his ability to speak, Tanner explained that he wanted the nurse to sit in on the evening's session.

"Good idea. I'm betting she's going to work out. She's only been here a few hours, but before Bert could get to the steps at the Anderson place, she found a hammer and nails and fixed them herself. Bert took her up to the clinic today. It's a little remote, you know, but that didn't faze her."

Tanner put an end to Carol's endorsement of someone he wished with all his heart he'd never met. "Her number. Do you have it?"

"The Andersons never had their phone shut off. That's where she's staying. Did I say that? I heard from Elizabeth last week," Carol went on. "They might have to sell the place. It's a shame. Maybe, if Phil's strong enough, they'll get up here this winter. He isn't recovering from that stroke the way they hoped he would."

Tanner hated hearing that. From what they'd told him, Phil and Elizabeth Anderson had fallen in love with the Mammoth area long before it became the skiing mecca it was now. They'd built the graceful, sturdy A-frame almost singlehandedly. Tanner had been one of those asked to share hot chocolate and conversation by the rock fireplace and look out at Lake Mary just beyond the floor-to-ceiling window.

Melaine would love it there.

Tanner managed to say a little more but cut off the conversation as soon as he could. He walked to his own oversize window and stared out. The Anderson place was situated almost directly across the lake from where he lived. It wasn't dark yet, but when it was, he would be able to see the A-frame's lights. And he'd be slammed up against the reality of Melaine Landa's reappearance in his life.

Tanner stabbed out Melaine's phone number. She answered before he'd finished a long, necessary breath. Tanner clenched his jaw until his muscles ached. It didn't help. He could still feel her. Smell her. Taste her. He wondered if she still wore her hair loose and soft-scented.

"Melaine? It's Tanner. Tanner Harris. Do you remember me?"

Silence. For four, maybe five seconds, silence. "Yes. I haven't . . . Tanner, Bert Edmonds told me you were here."

Tanner took another breath. "I take it you understand we're going to have to work together."

"I don't know how it can be avoided."

She didn't want this any more than he did. Good. That was the way things needed to be. "There's going to be a meeting tonight," he explained. "A training session for the new patrol members."

"You think I should be there?"

"That's why I'm calling. Otherwise . . ."

She remained silent for so long that the quiet tore into him. He needed to hear her voice again. Not want, *need*. "I understand," she finally said. The words weren't quite a whisper. "Otherwise you'd have never called me. Where? What time?"

Quickly and unemotionally, Tanner told her. He could

have hung up, but something about her voice held him. He remembered a gentle woman who spoke passionately of her love of nursing, and sunlight, and little else. Maybe that mysterious woman with her witch's spell still existed. The thought made him straighten and turn away from the lake. "Carol says you did some repairs at the Anderson place. I'm surprised it needed any."

"Just the porch. The weight of the snow buckled a step. You don't want to hear this, do you?"

He didn't. What he needed was to acknowledge that her voice still held a power on him, and then, somehow, free himself from that power. "You're lucky the Andersons decided to rent it out. A lot of people have been interested in the place."

"I love it. Tanner?"

Her voice hung in the air, swirled around him, entered him. Other women had spoken his name; surely one of those voices would have stayed with him. But they hadn't; Melaine Landa had been the only one who'd made his name sound like a lover's caress.

"What?"

"I don't know." She sighed, a veiled ripple of sound. "You're still doing what you were when we . . . I guess I should have considered the possibility that you might leave Squaw Valley and come here. You said you wanted to involve yourself with an expansion project. We . . . Tanner, we're going to have to talk."

"No we aren't." Anger plowed through him and allowed him to dismiss the fact that she remembered his need for new challenges. "It's all been said."

"You think so?"

"You lied."

"So you believed."

"What else would you call it?" Tanner prodded. "You told me there wasn't anyone in your life—and then I pick up the phone and find your husband on the other end."

Melaine had been standing, staring out at the shadows

that slowly turned Lake Mary from blue to dusky gray, but with Tanner's accusation, the strength went out of her. If he expected something in reply, she was sorry, but it simply wasn't in her to respond. From the moment she heard his voice, she'd been trapped with the awful memory of the light going out of a man's eyes and a receiver being slammed with such force that the instrument had been broken.

He had walked out on her, taking with him a lifeline when she'd believed herself drowning.

"Melaine."

"What? In an hour. I'll be there."

"If you'd rather not—"

"I'll be there."

Melaine hung up, hauled herself to her feet, and made her way to the sliding-glass door that led to a porch overlooking the gently rippling lake. She stepped outside, needing the cool breeze that came up from the dark water. How old had she been when she first came here? Twenty? Working at Mammoth those two, pine scented summers had provided her with a place to live and money she'd put away for the expenses her scholarships didn't cover.

Back then she'd had responsibilities that filled forty hours a week. The rest of the time had been hers. She'd been free to learn to fish, to borrow a canoe and drift from one end of the many mountain lakes to the other. She'd covered every marked trail and then took off cross-country to blaze her own route. When she wasn't working or exploring, she wrote her sisters and ran up a phone bill she cold scarce afford.

Those years were behind her, just as were the uncertain early ones when she'd been her sisters' protector and parent. Now Melaine was a nurse with five years of experience under her belt and an opportunity for advancement that hadn't been possible within the confines of a Sacramento hospital.

The only thing that stood between Melaine and that dream was Tanner Harris.

A little daylight still touched the sky when Melaine completed the mile-long drive on the dirt and gravel road that circled Lake Mary. A few pockets of snow clung to deeply shadowed valleys near the top of the surrounding mountains, but at this altitude, the land was summer dry, summer lazy.

As she reached Tanner's cabin, she saw two casually dressed young men bound up the stairs and walk inside without knocking. A truck carrying three more men pulled in behind her before she could get out of her car.

Although it was larger than the cabins rented out to vacationers, the outer walls of Tanner's place had the same rough finish, steps made of stone, a wood shake roof. Close to the foundation, she spotted a number of small holes, openings to underground homes for chipmunks.

"You're the nurse?" a redhead with a full beard asked. "I thought you'd be a lot older."

Melaine smiled. "I'm twenty-eight. Sometimes I feel as if I'm at least a hundred and twenty. Does that help?"

One of the other men shoved his buddy aside. "Don't mind Red. He has all the diplomacy of a grizzly. Welcome aboard."

Swept along by the three young men, Melaine entered Tanner's home. The cabin smelled of pitch and lumber, wool and wilderness. Like her place, the living area was dominated by a fireplace. She remembered that he loved working with wood. There was no mistaking the painstaking workmanship in the large coffee table created from an oak burl, the solid couch fashioned from rough-finished mahogany and polished until the grain stood out against the leather fabric. The oil painting of Mammoth Mountain lit by unobtrusive lighting acted as a focal point for the room.

Tanner wasn't here. Melaine could hear voices in the

kitchen. Still, she hesitated when the three young men made their way toward the sounds of activity. Instead, she stood alone, soaking in the cabin owner's essence, understanding that this and not one of the new, modern places closer to civilization was where Tanner belonged.

"We're going to be getting started in a minute."

She turned slowly. Tanner hadn't aged. Although it made no sense, and she wanted to deny it, Melaine remembered every line, every angle of the man standing in the doorway between kitchen and living room. There was nothing that could easily be labeled handsome about his six-foot-one-inch frame; he was too coarse-finished for that. Yet, his proud ruggedness had once drawn her to him, and if she didn't remain on guard, it might claim her again.

This was a black-haired, gray-eyed man with large hands, shoulders with the width needed for the responsibility he'd assumed, legs both long and heavily muscled. No matter how quickly the snows fell, or how fierce the winter wind blew, if she touched his cheek, she believed she'd tap the warmth in him. Maybe the sun had made a permanent impact on his flesh, and maybe it was simply that there was that much life within him.

Tanner needed a haircut. And a shave. The dim lighting only added to the dark shadows buried in his eyes. Those shadows reached out and fashioned a barrier between them.

Melaine fought the need to fold her hands into fists as protection against what she'd just discovered. "I like your place," she told him, her voice carefully neutral. "It's right for you."

"How do you know what's right for me?"

He wanted to attack her. Despite the pain, at least Melaine now understood the rules. "Maybe you're right," she said softly. "We weren't together long enough for that. But I remember certain things. You work with wood because you don't like anything artificial."

"Artificiality? Yeah. I have this thing about the truth."

The truth. Bracing herself, Melaine continued to meet his eyes. Still, it was a moment before she could make herself speak. "If you want, I'll tell you everything."

"I don't want. It's history. Remember that, history. We're sitting out on my rear deck, Mrs. Landa. There isn't anything to drink except beer."

"Tanner . . . All right. Beer it is." Without waiting for him to surrender his position by the doorway, Melaine walked past him and into the kitchen. She grabbed a beer from the open cooler on the counter and followed the sounds out the back door. The oak deck overlooking Lake Mary had been illuminated by several kerosene lamps that nudged at the night with rose-tinted fingers. The seated men and two women were already looking through their manuals. Melaine found a canvas-backed chair and lowered herself into it. She wasn't sure what had prompted her to accept Tanner's offer of a beer. Offer? No. She couldn't call what he'd flung at her that. He'd issued a challenge, one she didn't dare ignore.

Tanner sat across from her. His eyes met hers, and for a moment Melaine fought a silent battle with him. When, finally, he broke contact, she didn't feel the victor. Neither did she believe she'd been vanquished. Instead, the necessary confrontation had simply been postponed.

There was little for Melaine to contribute to Tanner's thorough, rapid-fire presentation. He might be only thirty-four, but his career had given him a wealth of experience. His review of how to handle shock victims exhibiting a variety of injuries went further than checking for dilated pupils, shallow, irregular breathing, and keeping the victim quiet until a detailed assessment could be made. Tanner explained that he was just as concerned with the condition of those providing first aid.

"We average three hundred fifty inches of snow a year," he said. "That ups the odds that you'll work in a storm. You're going to be concentrating on the victim, keeping him or her warm and immobile, giving directions to the rest of the rescue team, maybe having to calm other skiers. Believe me, you're going to forget about yourself. That's dangerous. If you wind up with hypothermia on the top of Grizzly, you aren't going to be any help to the fool with a broken ankle.''

Someone asked Tanner about storm predictability. He detailed the area's reliance on the national weather service and then, before Melaine could prepare for it, the tone that would have done a teacher proud, became somber. "Storms are easy to deal with. It's the other that keeps us on our toes."

"The other?" the man asked, but Melaine didn't wait for Tanner to answer.

"Earthquakes," she said softly. "And avalanches triggered by an earthquake."

For a moment there was only Tanner's eyes meeting hers and the stripping away of three years. He respected her knowledge; at least he gave her that. "Mrs. Landa is right," Tanner said. "This is earthquake country. Just ask the residents of San Francisco. We're tapped into seismologists throughout the state, but for the most part, that's only going to tell us how big a quake was, not allow us to accurately predict when, or even *if* it's coming."

"But we can take some precautions, can't we?" someone asked.

"We wouldn't be worth our salaries if we didn't. That's why we can't allow heavy snow buildup around the runs. As long as we regularly blast those areas, we'll be able to keep hot spots to a minimum. But like I said, an earthquake's unpredictable. There's no way we can plan for all eventualities."

Melaine nodded. "Which means I—and the rest of the medical community—have to be just as, if not more, prepared than you men in order to deal with multiple traumas."

"That's right," Tanner added. "An essential part of the

system here is emergency preparedness. There's a complex communication network between search and rescue, the clinic, hospital, police, you name it. That's why I asked Mrs. Landa to join us. She needs to know what we're doing, just as we need to be familiar with her role."

There was no longer any light left in the sky. In a few minutes the stars would make an appearance, but for now there were only the flickering lights from the kerosene lamps. The faces of the men and women had been cast in red-hued shadows, Tanner's perhaps the deepest. His compassion, his devotion to the safety of others was borne out in his strong and yet quiet voice, the medical facts so deeply ingrained that he hadn't once looked at his manual. Despite herself, Melaine leaned forward, intent on what he said as his words laced a trail through the wind skittering in the treetops.

You're incredible. The most incredible woman I've ever known.

Melaine had never been told that before, never believed herself capable of wringing such emotion from a man. But something in her had touched certain cords in Tanner Harris, just as something in him touched her.

They'd met on the beach of Lake Tahoe, a chance meeting of eyes, a conversation that began with the inconsequential, but quickly became something vital. Tanner told her he was taking a short break from nearby Squaw Valley. He loved what he did. He just wanted more—new challenges, new demands. It was, he admitted with a quick smile, hard being a latter-day Indiana Jones. When he asked what brought her to the cold, clear lake, Melaine sketched her evolution from naive college student to a nurse trying to decide her next career move. She didn't tell him why she was living in Nevada.

After hours of talking and lounging on the beach, they'd gone in search of dinner. It hadn't been a date; it hadn't been not a date. Neither of them put more than a half dozen coins in the casino slot machines. Instead they'd been drawn to the performing groups, talking, reaching beyond the point of being strangers. Until 4 A.M., Tanner and Melaine listened to the slender reed of a woman with a rich, guttural voice, a trio of guitarists capable of producing sounds that sawed and vibrated through the audience. They listened to comics, watched costumed dancers, and went back to the woman with the incredible voice.

For the first two nights Tanner and Melaine parted to grab a few hours of sleep and then met for breakfast. On the third night no questions were asked. They went to her place because it was closer to the lake and because Melaine, although she didn't tell Tanner this, needed to be near her phone.

In Tanner's arms, Melaine found a few hours of renewal.

Until that fateful phone call.

The EMTs started getting to their feet. Melaine had no idea how long she'd been sitting, only that what remained of her beer was the same temperature as her hand. The night air felt cold on her spine. She repeated that she wanted to acquaint the patrol members with her facilities and assured them that, although she wasn't an expert skier, she could tackle the majority of runs.

"You do much cross-country skiing?" the big redhead asked as they reentered Tanner's kitchen. "That's the only way to go."

Before she could explain that she preferred that to downhill, someone argued that cross-country skiing, while fine if you wanted to get away from it all, was tame compared to attacking a steep slope at dawn after a fresh snowfall.

"I did that once," Melaine admitted, smiling at the memory. "It started out perfect. Only, it started snowing again. Before I reached the bottom, I couldn't see two feet in front of me and looked like a giant snowball. I swear my nose took three days to thaw."

The redhead nodded energetically. "You ever been frostbit? Lord, that hurts!"

Melaine was about to answer when Tanner walked into the kitchen. He brought with him size and brooding shadows that stripped her of her ability to think. She felt his eyes rake a hostile path down her body. His gaze lingered on her legs, then came up, touching hips, waist, breasts. Finally, his nails slicing the way, he rammed his hands in his back pockets. "Where's Chris?"

It took every shred of self-control for Melaine to face Tanner's accusation. "Chris is part of the past, Tanner."

"Is he?"

The redheaded giant stared, obviously aware that something more than a casual exchange was taking place. "Yes," she said in a voice so calm she couldn't quite believe it belonged to her. "I talked to him a few days before I came here. He approves of what I'm doing."

"Does he? I wouldn't think—"

Melaine didn't care whether Tanner finished. Ignoring him, she turned away, put down her beer, and headed for the living room. She wanted nothing more than to get in her car and go home.

Tanner followed her onto the porch and then down the stairs. He was only a few feet behind when she opened the car door and slid in.

"It won't work."

"What won't?" She should have wound up her window. That way she wouldn't have to listen to him.

"Your car. It'll never get you up to the clinic in the winter."

"I know," Melaine said on the tail of a breath heavy with relief. Driving through snow was a subject she could deal with. "Bert's going to let me use his Jeep."

"The heater isn't much."

"I won't be in it long."

"What's he like, Melaine?"

Danger! The alarm shot through her, warning her to move slowly. "Bert? You know him better than I do."

"No." When Tanner shook his head, she lost contact with his eyes. It was safer, maybe easier this way. "Not Bert," he went on. "Chris. What's your husband like?"

"Ex-husband," Melaine said with her heart ice-coated and her stomach knotted and hard.

"Why? Didn't he like his wife running around on him?"

The ice coating wasn't thick enough; Tanner was still capable of inflicting pain. Now Melaine's legs and arms felt on fire. If it hadn't been for the warning vibrating through her, she would have forced the car to life and fled. "I didn't run around on him, Tanner. No matter what you think, whether you believe me, that's the truth."

"The hell. You—"

Melaine rammed the key in the ignition. The engine's roar drowned out his voice. "You didn't try to understand three years ago. Why should it be different now?" she shot at him.

"No reason, Mrs. Landa. No reason at all."

What little sense of victory Tanner gained from Melaine's sharp intake of breath lasted less time than it did for her to back out of his drive. Tanner felt like a bastard, a spiteful, vindictive bastard, and that wasn't the way he lived his life.

But Melaine Landa had touched him, and then hurt him, in ways he hadn't believed possible. When he'd realized the extent of her deception, all he wanted was to put the experience behind him. Only, walking out on her hadn't worked then.

And it wasn't working now.

THREE

The A-frame which earlier had so intrigued Melaine barely earned a glance. It was almost 9 P.M., too early to go to bed, yet too late for anything except slipping out of her clothes and into a cotton lounging outfit.

Her thoughts were full of Tanner. Her entire being was full of him, and his harsh dismissal hurt. She could think of only one way to get him out of her mind—talking to Amber.

The eight-year-old girl answered the phone, her voice sounding slightly hollowed out, as if more than forty miles separated them. "Melaine! You're really there?"

"I'm really here, honey. How are you doing?"

"Great. I was scared you might have to stay in Sacramento after all."

"Well, I didn't, did I?" Melaine asked. She closed her eyes so she could better picture the blond, coltish girl—and battle her tears. "I told them I *had* to have the job because of you. So? What have you been up to? Have you met any of the kids you'll be going to school with?"

A few, Amber told her. Melaine wasn't surprised. Despite Amber's unconventional homelife, she had a healthy self-image and easily reached beyond herself. Melaine hoped she was at least partially responsible. Certainly she'd done everything she could to make Amber believe in herself.

"It's summer," Amber explained in response to Melaine's suggestion that maybe she should be thinking about going to bed. "I can sleep in as long as I want. Guess what? I'm going to get to ride in a Camaro, a red one."

Melaine pulled on a slipper one-handed. "Your dad has a new car?"

"No. He says he has to finish paying for the van first. Pete. You know, the new teacher at day care. Pete goes to college. He's going to be a . . . I forget. He likes skiing and movies about horses, just like me, and he makes every kind of pizza you can think of. Pete plays football. He said maybe all the kids at the center can come watch him. What does it mean to ride the wood?"

Judging from the adoration she heard in Amber's voice, Melaine decided not to tell her that her hero might be a bench warmer. Instead she asked for more information about the red Camaro. According to Amber, Pete wasn't happy with the way the car ran, but Amber thought it "hot." Pete had let her sit behind the wheel.

Melaine laughed at Amber's newest buzz word; her laugh was tempered by the weight of what she'd borne for so long. If only she could reach out and draw the child to her! Thank God, Bishop was less than an hour's drive from Mammoth. As soon as she'd settled in at her job, she'd head south. She'd hug and kiss, and pretend not to notice how much Amber had grown in the month since she'd seen her.

And, if it was all right with Chris, Amber could come here for a few days. They'd go fishing, just the two of them. Amber gave the suggestion a resounding "all right!" As long as she didn't have to touch a worm, she'd stay out in a boat all day. No worms, Melaine promised, her mouth curving into a smile.

Melaine told Amber about the chair lifts and trams that marched up to the top of the mountain. It would make for a spectacular ride. "I met a woman who rents out horses," she added. "I think she has one just right for you."

"What's its name?"

"Rabbit. Carol says she calls him that because he jumped all over the place when he was a colt."

"Rabbit? That's weird."

The easygoing conversation faltered when Melaine asked where Chris was. Amber wasn't sure. Daddy had called earlier to say he would be late getting home, but that was all right because Mrs. McKinsey and her baby were here to keep her company. "I don't think I like Jeffrey right now," Amber admitted. "Mrs. McKinsey says he's getting his teeth, and sometimes it hurts. All he does is cry. I didn't cry like that when I was a baby, did I?"

"Of course not. We won't talk about when you were two, all right? I won't remind you that I had to hang all the furniture from the ceiling to keep it safe."

Amber giggled. "But you didn't mind 'cause you love me."

"That's right," Melaine said softly. "You had me wrapped around your little finger."

Amber giggled again. "You wouldn't fit. I fixed dinner—toasted cheese sandwiches just like you taught me. Now we're watching wrestling."

"Wrestling? Honey, none of that's real. You understand that, don't you?"

"Sure. But it's funny. One man has this big old snake. And this other wrestler has his girlfriend with him. She tries to run around on her high heels, but she isn't very fast."

Melaine groaned. The housekeeper was a bit of a free spirit, with a husband who was absent more often than on the scene. Melaine didn't particularly approve of Amber watching professional wrestling, but it wasn't her place to impose rules. For a few minutes she let Amber explain the action while she made sure the child understood that the screams and blood-letting were as carefully choreographed as a detective-show fight scene. At last, mindful of the long-distance charges, Melaine again brought up the hour, and buoyed by a heartfelt "I love you!" from Amber, hung up.

The house felt even more empty than it had a few minutes before, forcing Melaine back on her feet and outside. Taking a job within easy driving distance of Amber was supposed to make things easier for both of them. But at least in Sacramento Melaine had had supportive people around her. She'd confided in several of the other nurses about her unique situation, and their input had made weathering the empty feeling a little more bearable.

Was there anyone here she could talk to about the pain of not getting a bear hug whenever she needed one?

Whoever had begun the job of ordering supplies must have assumed that most of the clinic's business would be emergency medicine, but after giving it some thought the next morning, Melaine was certain she'd get a lot of drop-in traffic ranging from sore throats and colds to blisters. Although she would have to get her expenditures approved by the committee in charge of budgets, Melaine hoped they would agree that a few colorful prints on the walls, light reading materials, and a tape player so she could play easy-listening music would help the clinic's image. She'd turn into an emergency nurse the moment a call came in. In the meantime, she wanted people to realize that their sore muscles would be taken seriously, but not too seriously.

Melaine was in the middle of stocking a shelf with gauze and bandages when she heard her first official patient. According to Carol Edmonds, who clumped in with a disgusted look, she had been instructing a middle-aged woman in how to mount a horse when the tenderfoot lost her balance. Carol had been knocked against a wooden fence and now sported a large splinter embedded in her forearm.

"I didn't let anyone know," Carol explained after showing Melaine the red, swollen flesh around the dark sliver. "I braved things out until I got that blasted woman on Trixie. Then I tried to pull it out, but it's really in there."

"It certainly is." Melaine indicated that Carol was to sit on the examining table. "I'm afraid I'm going to have to do a little digging."

"Dig away."

Melaine laughed. "Want a bullet to bite? We do have some marvelous innovations these days that'll take away all feeling."

Sheepishly, Carol nodded. "I don't know what gets into me sometimes. I guess it comes from looking like an ox. People expect me to be strong."

"You don't look like an ox," Melaine told her as she prepared a shot of novocaine. Despite Carol's substantial frame, Carol carried herself like a dancer. Yes, she single-handedly ran an equestrian business and competently handled the rigors of winter in an isolated resort, but there was a femininity to Carol that made Melaine forget that the other woman outweighed her by some thirty pounds.

"I guess I could have gone to the hospital to have this worked on, but I wanted to see how things were coming along here," Carol explained. "The way Bert goes on about the place, you'd think he was the architect instead of the builder. He thinks all these windows are nothing short of the brainchild of a genius. You aren't having second thoughts, are you? I mean, it's going to be a lot of responsibility."

"I want the responsibility." Melaine leaned over Carol's arm. "After years of saying 'Yes, Doctor,' I love the idea of being in charge. As to whether it'll all work smoothly—that remains to be seen."

"You have good support."

"If you mean the community, you're right. Everyone's been so helpful."

"I mean Tanner."

Melaine had the tweezers firmly around the splinter. She'd been ready to ease it out; now she had to take a breath and steady her hand before she could complete the action. "Tanner?"

"You met him last night, remember."

There. The splinter was out. "How did you know that?"

"Red came by after the meeting. That kid. This is the first time he's really been away from home. He gets homesick and hangs out around our place until we kick him out. Anyway, Red asked if we thought he was too young for you. When I pointed out that you couldn't possibly be interested in someone who hadn't figured out how a washing machine works, he said it was probably a lost cause anyway because there was some kind of something between you and Tanner."

Melaine tried to busy herself with cleaning the wound, but the process didn't command her full attention. "No. You're wrong."

"How do you know? Hey, I might be an old married lady, but that doesn't mean I don't have eyes. Tanner Harris is one fine-looking man."

"I know." The words were out before Melaine could stop them.

"See." Carol laughed, and turned her arm so she would have a better view of what Melaine was doing. "I knew you were aware—"

"Carol." Melaine stopped her. "Believe me, Tanner isn't interested in me. And I'm not interested in him."

Carol looked as if she'd been told that the family picnic had been canceled. "You're sure you won't reconsider? Romances are so much fun to watch."

Melaine almost smiled. It was a warm afternoon; she had the clinic door open. The air smelled clean enough to chase away any and all dark moods. As long as she thought about a blue sky and fishing with Amber, she would remain optimistic about life. "I'm sorry to disappoint you. Look, I had to do a little cutting here. I'd like you to keep the bandage on for a few days and come back if it shows any signs of getting infected."

"It won't." Carol squirmed, obviously in a hurry to put an end to being a patient. "Look, if I ask you a question, will you promise to keep it to yourself?"

Puzzled, Melaine nodded.

"Good." Carol looked out the window, down at her hands, and then finally back at Melaine. "If a woman was to need a little maternity support, is that something you could do?"

"You're pregnant?"

Carol blushed. "Maybe. I've been thinking, well, you know with all this business about malpractice insurance and doctors not wanting to get involved with delivering babies because of it, maybe the hospital doctors don't want me. Besides, I think maybe I'd like to see a woman. Isn't that crazy? I mean, a doctor's a doctor, right. It shouldn't bother me having a man—"

"You're babbling," Melaine broke in. "How about if I ask a couple of questions. You said maybe you're pregnant?"

Although Melaine wasn't quite finished taping the bandage in place, Carol slid off the examination table. "It isn't a maybe. I mean, I'm regular as clockwork, and I was supposed to have my period three weeks ago."

Melaine grabbed Carol's hand, holding her in place so she could finish covering the wound. "What's wrong?"

"Wrong?"

"Wrong," Melaine repeated. "You're uptight. If you're pregnant, and if I'm going to be working with you, I have to know what's going on. What about Bert? How does he feel about becoming a father?"

Carol sagged against the gleaming table. "I don't know.

I mean, we've talked about babies, and he says he's all for it, but, well, Bert's forty-two. He's never had children. What if—well, what if he doesn't have the energy for them?"

"Bert? Not have the energy? That man can work circles around men half his age."

Carol's slight smile told Melaine she agreed. "I know. But a baby. That's different. He's used to our being able to go anywhere at the drop of a hat, getting a full night's sleep, interrupting it for, you know, whenever the impulse strikes. If there's a baby—"

Again Melaine stopped Carol's chatter. "If there's a child, it'll become part of your life. You'll adjust."

Carol sagged against a counter. "I'm scared."

"Of having a baby?"

"Of course not. I'll probably spit it out and go right back to work. My mother had five kids and never lost a beat."

"Then—"

"You don't have children, do you? Of course you don't, or they'd be with you. What I'm scared of—you promise you won't tell anyone this—is maybe I'm not good mother material."

Casting aside her reaction to Carol's question about her having children, Melaine took the other woman's hands. "Listen to me. Please. There isn't a woman alive who knows the answer to that until they have a child to raise. Motherhood, parenthood, I firmly believe it's instinct. Either you have it, or you don't."

"You really believe that?"

"Yes. I do." Melaine paused, weighing the wisdom of what she was about to say. Last night she'd wished she had a friend to talk to. Carol had just exposed something deeply personal; she could do the same. "I'd like to tell you something . . ." Melaine began. "My mother had three children, all girls and all close together. She wasn't cut out for that role. It was . . . I think maybe she saw motherhood as a trick someone played on her. She tried. It just didn't work."

"I'm sorry."

Melaine gave Carol an uneven smile. "So am I. For her sake. And for the sake of the children she had. Carol, I honestly don't believe it's going to be like that for you. Think of the way you relate to your horses. And you genuinely like people. I sensed that the moment we met."

"That's easy. My friends don't ask me to walk the floor with them. And the horses—I don't have to make sure they grow up moral and responsible."

"True." Melaine stifled another grin. "Carol, what you're saying, your fears, that's to be expected."

"Maybe."

A truck approached the clinic, its tires spinning a little on the loose gravel. After a moment, Melaine went on. "A woman who doesn't question her ability to be a good mother is the one who's in trouble. I've seen it enough times through work." *Through personal experience.* "You have almost nine months to get ready for this adventure. So does Bert."

"I—haven't told him."

"Then do it, and I'll see you tomorrow."

"All right." Carol stared down at her broad hands. "A baby. In a few months, I'm going to hold my very own baby."

Melaine turned away, willing herself to concentrate on putting away bandages and sterilizing the tweezers. She didn't face Carol again until the mountain breeze had dried her tears.

There were no longer any lights on in the clinic. Still, as Tanner rode the tram down the mountain, his thoughts were pulled, unbidden, to where Melaine would spend her days for as long as she lived at Mammoth. The wind had kicked up this afternoon, ruffling Tanner's hair and filling him with restlessness. He'd spent the day on one of the higher runs, grooming it for winter's activity. He should be interested in nothing except a shower and dinner with one of the other ski patrol members.

Damn it, she had no right coming here. Mammoth was his. He knew its mountains and valleys, the gentle beginner slopes, the steep runs reserved for experts, those menacing areas where snow could accumulate and break free, cascading over the unwary if he and the rest of the team didn't render that terrain impotent by blasting. In this world he was in control, at least as much in control as nature would allow.

But Melaine had come here, threatening to undermine everything he'd worked for since walking out on her.

She'd said she wasn't married anymore. Had what's his name . . . Chris—had Chris given up on this devil in angel's guise?

Hell, it didn't matter.

Hours later after good food and good conversation, Tanner returned to his cabin. He walked out onto the porch that extended to the edge of the lake, looked across at the distant lights, and faced the truth. It did matter. Melaine would never be out of his system unless he confronted her. Until they'd put the past, and what they'd shared, behind them. Grunting, Tanner spun around and headed inside. He flipped on a lamp and dialed the Andersons' place—her place.

Melaine's "hello" reached him, sweet and open. The mesmerizing tone didn't change until he identified himself. Then he sensed her draw into herself. "No," she responded to his question. "I wasn't in bed. What do you want?"

"Some answers."

"Answers? I thought you didn't want anything to do with me."

"I don't. It would suit me just fine if you were still wherever you came from. What happened to Nevada?"

"Nevada was never my home, Tanner. I was there . . .

I'm sorry if you don't want me here, but I'm not going to leave."

"I figured that out." Unbelievably, he was glad to hear that. It must be part of the spell she'd cast over him. Part of the mystique that had nothing to do with reality. "That's why I called. Unfinished business."

"What do you want me to say? That I'm sorry? I am. More than you'll ever know."

"Are you?" Could he hurt her? Despite the expanse separating them, despite the impersonality of a phone call, could he hurt her? Did he want to? "I don't have a clue what you were thinking back then. That's what keeps digging at me, realizing I didn't understand you at all. But maybe that doesn't matter to you."

"Do you believe that?"

Her question and the soft sigh that went with it distracted Tanner. "Good question. That's why I called. To find out where we're going."

"We aren't going anywhere."

Her voice shouldn't be this familiar to him. She couldn't possibly have this much of an impact on him. And yet he could imagine her mouth and throat working, the way her nose flared when words were spoken with passion. Damn it, she'd remembered that he loved working with wood and built his own furniture. "What was it? A fling? Separate vacations so you could see what you could dig up without your husband in tow? Is that something the two of you do—did? Each of you off prowling? What did you do when those vacations were over, compare notes?"

"You wouldn't let me explain then," Melaine said finally, her voice not rising above a whisper. "Why is it different now?"

"It just is."

"I need more than that, Tanner. I was in so much pain back then. I don't want to have to relive it unless there's some reason."

She'd been in pain? Tanner closed his eyes, fighting

waves of something he didn't want to feel. "My right to know isn't enough?"

"Rights? You walked out on me."

"You think I shouldn't have? When I pick up a phone and find my . . . *lover's* husband on the other end of the line—"

Melaine had pulled the phone away from her mouth. He could hear the fading away of her voice. "I won't talk to you like this, Tanner," she whispered. "You say you want the truth, but you're twisting things around. You want me to feel dirty. I can't. I won't."

Tanner was listening to dead air. For a moment he considered redialing and demanding they have this out, but he didn't. Instead he hung up the phone and walked back outside, breathing deeply of clean mountain air. Across Lake Mary, a single light flickered. Or maybe he was capable of noticing only that one light.

Damn it, she was the one who'd inflicted the wound. What did she expect him to do, pretend they hadn't made love? Act as if they hadn't met, never said, done—

Only, wrenching the truth out of her wouldn't change one simple fact. There wasn't anything left between them.

Bert wouldn't take no for an answer. "If we don't go now, they might be gone," the builder and pilot explained when Melaine picked up the clinic phone the next afternoon. "I tried to reach Carol, but she's out with some tourists riding over the June Lake Falls. Tanner's tied up with someone from the forest service. I've never seen that many mule deer together. It'll blow your mind."

"I'm sure it will." Melaine held the phone a few inches from her ear as defense against Bert's excitement. "But you just got back. Are you sure you want to go flying again?"

"Would I be calling if I didn't? Come on. It won't take that long for you to hightail it over to the airport. You'll be back at work in a couple of hours, and even if you aren't, wouldn't you rather see a four-hundred-pound buck than count tongue depressors? I've got my camera and a new telephoto lens, but I can't fly and take pictures at the same time."

Another load of supplies had arrived this morning, and Melaine had barely made a dent in the unpacking. But a mule deer with magnificent antlers and a flight over mountains, valleys, and lakes couldn't help but lift her mood. Besides, if the pictures turned out, she could have one blown up for Amber. After being assured that the herd included a half dozen or so of last spring's fawns, Melaine told Bert she'd meet him as soon as possible. She locked the clinic and got into her car without looking up at the mountain where Tanner and the other members of the ski team might be.

Bert was right. The short flight was worth it. The light plane made little noise as it skimmed close to the treetops. While Melaine peered out the windows, Bert told her about the days when he thought he wanted to be a commercial pilot. "I figured, wearing a uniform, taking responsibility for hundreds of people and millions of dollars' worth of planes, that's what I wanted," he explained. "I stuck it out for almost five years until I woke up in some motel room with absolutely no idea whether I was on the West or East Coast. I turned in my resignation a week later."

Melaine stared down at rolling hills dotted with evergreens and then over at a hawk skimming along the horizon. She felt incredibly free. "How did you meet Carol?"

"She was my parents' neighbor. Back then she was working at a riding stable and hating it. Mom was always saying I should ask Carol out, but I'd seen too many long-distance romances go down the tubes. I dropped by to tell my folks about quitting my job, and she showed up to mow their lawn. I figured, after the way she took care of their yard, the least I could do was marry her."

Melaine didn't try to hide her grin. "Certainly. There's nothing else you could have done."

"Come to think of it, maybe she asked me. I don't remember." Bert pointed ahead. "Okey, this is Round Valley. I spotted the herd up near the north end. The does and fawns were grazing while the bucks stalked them. It's the breeding season, you know. Some of those bucks—when their chests and necks get thick, it's an incredible sight."

The herd wasn't where Bert had spotted it earlier, but the deer hadn't moved far. Although at first Melaine didn't see any bucks, she was treated to a view of a dozen does and their half-grown fawns grazing at the south edge of the valley. Then, when she'd gone through half a roll of film, a single buck, followed a minute later by two others, stepped out of the trees.

The sight wiped everything else from Melaine's mind. She'd seen deer before, of course, but there was something humbling about watching the magnificent, heavy-bodied bucks walking proud and purposeful. The animals were huge, each with a great rack that looked so heavy she was surprised they were able to lift their heads. All of the deer were sleek and healthy with thick coats that would protect them through the long winter. The herd ignored the little plane, the fawns grazing and playing by turn, the does aware of little except their suitors.

Melaine pointed Bert's camera at the largest buck. "You think he weighs four hundred pounds?"

"Maybe a little more. They're in prime shape right now. Give them a few weeks. By the time they've finished chasing the does around, they'll have lost a lot of weight. Those deer come from Yosemite and aren't hunted so they get some real size to them."

Melaine wasn't sure the weight loss would take a couple of weeks. Although they tried to chase each other off, the bucks were also intent on singling out certain does and enticing them into the woods. By the time the largest buck and a doe with a scar on her left flank disappeared from view, Melaine was into her second roll of film.

"Thank you. That was wonderful," she whispered when Bert finally turned the plane around. "You didn't have to do this for me, but I'm glad you did."

"I figured you needed it."

"You did?"

"Yep. Cooped up in that clinic all day. Besides, I kinda wanted to have a little time alone with you."

Melaine put away the camera. "Oh?"

"To talk about Carol. She came to see you yesterday."

Melaine nodded. They were over the trees again; beyond that she could see the high eastern California desert. Someday, somehow, she would share this with Amber.

"I knew something was on her mind. I just never figured it was, you know. Carol says she can't believe you don't have children. She says you understand that becoming a parent isn't as cut and dried as they try to make us think. She's grateful you didn't tell her she had no business having mixed feelings."

"How do you feel about it?" Melaine asked. "Becoming a father's going to mean a big change for you."

"Tell me about it." Bert glanced at Melaine before again concentrating on flying. "I knew Carol wanted children. We talked about it before we got married. It sounded exciting in the abstract, if you know what I mean. But I'm an old man. Old for taking care of babies."

"You're hardly going to be the world's oldest father."

"But I've had more than forty years to run my life the way I want. If she hadn't been as independent as she is, if she'd been one of those women who lives in her husband's shadow, I don't think I would have married Carol. A baby—a baby isn't independent."

"No," Melaine agreed as they approached the airport. "A baby isn't. They need guidance, security, people who show them that they're worthwhile human beings. Bert,

I'm not going to tell you it'll be easy. But, like Carol, you have the capacity for love. I think that's the only base you'll need. Just be there for your children. Hold them and love them. Mostly love them. I've seen so many sick children get well simply because someone gave them TLC."

"Is that what your father did?"

Melaine met Bert's eyes. "My parents divorced when I was six. I never see him." Her simple words earned her a sharp look from Bert, but they were coming in to land, and he had work to do.

Melaine had gotten out of the plane before Bert opened his door and leaned out so she could hear him over the idling engine. "I'm sorry about your father. If you want to talk about that—"

Melaine reached up and ran her hand over Bert's chin. "Thank you, but it happened a long time ago. If you want to talk, about Carol and the baby, your feelings, anything—I don't pretend to have all the answers, but I can listen."

"What is this? Our own mutual support group?"

With the sun in her face and her mind full of memories of the deer they'd seen, Melaine laughed. "It sounds good to me. I'm glad I met you."

"And I'm glad Carol's going to be seeing you."

Melaine was still smiling as she walked away from the slowly moving plane. Bert had said he would have the pictures developed before the end of the week. They'd get together, and she could decide which ones she wanted.

Hers wasn't the only vehicle parked near the east end of the small airstrip. Even with the sun glinting off the vehicle, Melaine recognized Tanner's truck. With a short nod, she acknowledged the man leaning against it but didn't stop.

"You move fast."

Melaine had only the dimmest hint of what Tanner was talking about. The warm memory of the time she'd spent with Bert was still foremost in her thoughts. She didn't want that changed. "What are you doing here?"

"Picking up a forest ranger. Interesting about getting somewhere early. You get to see all kinds of things."

The day no longer felt warm. "What kind of things?"

"You and Bert. Damn it, Melaine. He's married."

"Bert and me?" How could she have once believed Tanner might give her a reason to want to go on living? He did nothing but tear at her. "He took me to see a deer herd."

"And you thanked him by kissing him."

"Kissing. I didn't—"

"Close enough."

"Stop it!" Melaine knotted her hands by her sides, her body wire taut. "Just stop and listen to me for a minute. Bert and I shared something special. I felt close to him. That's why I touched him, as a friend. Believe me, it's the only reason."

"Yeah?"

"Tanner, I'm not what you think I am. I'm sorry I didn't tell you everything, but—"

"Everything? You didn't tell me *anything*."

There wasn't any purpose in continuing this conversation. Tanner had judged, and found her guilty. Still, the better part of a minute passed before Melaine could tear her eyes free from his steady gaze and start for her car. She felt his eyes on her back, felt his anger. She accepted his hostility because she had no choice.

FOUR

For the rest of the afternoon, Melaine focused on the memory of the mule deer she and Bert had seen. Amber would love the pictures, of course, but to actually watch the deer in their natural surroundings would be a once-in-a-lifetime experience. If at all possible, she'd get Bert to take Amber flying before winter. It wasn't until she was locking up that Melaine faced facts. She'd concentrated on Amber and deer because that was easier than braving Tanner's harsh words.

Only, it couldn't continue like this. They would have to work with each other as long as they both lived at Mammoth Lakes. For the sake of their individual career commitments as well as consideration for those around them, she would have to make him listen.

He might not forgive her. She couldn't bear responsibility for that. But at least by the time she was done, he'd know the truth.

Instead of heading home, Melaine drove to Tanner's cabin. She wasn't sure he'd be there yet, but his truck was parked out front. As she got out, she heard the faint sound of music coming from an open window. What kind did he like?

Distracted by the thought of how little she knew about

him, Melaine walked up the steps and knocked on the front door.

"One sec," he called out. "Minor emergency."

Melaine stood, a mixture of fear and determination washing through her. She heard Tanner's solid footsteps as he stomped around. She'd almost given up on him when he yanked open the door. "Ground squirrel," he muttered, his head turned back toward the house's interior. "Don't ask me how he got inside . . . What are you doing here?"

Because she'd prepared herself for this reaction, Melaine was able to weather the quick change from his amusement to the closing down of all emotion. Still, she mourned the loss of the laughter which had shone in his eyes. "We have to talk."

"I don't think so."

"Tanner, please don't. I see you as a man who faces life head on. You don't back down from a demanding job. Why won't you hear me out?"

Tanner jammed his hands in his pockets and rocked back onto his heels. "You want to bring up history. I don't."

"I don't think we have any choice. Tanner, I want to tell you some things. I have to. Then you can decide where we're going."

"*We* aren't going anywhere."

"I know that," she said too quickly. "But professionally—"

"Professionally we'll each do our jobs. That's the only thing that matters."

"Is it?" Melaine challenged. He was making this so damn hard. "What if we can't talk to each other? What if this barrier, this misunderstanding remains? It's going to color the way we approach our jobs. And if someone's safety is at stake—"

"You call it a misunderstanding? Come on, Melaine, it's a hell of a lot more than that."

She lifted her chin. "Yes. I guess it is. But you'll never be able to judge that if you don't know—everything."

"And you're not going to give up until then, are you?"

"I can't."

"Can't you? All right. You're here. Get it out. Over and done with." Tight-lipped, Tanner stepped back to let her in.

She slipped past him, aware of the warm, masculine scent lingering on him. His day had been physical, but then everything about him was physical. Despite her need to concentrate on him, Melaine looked around as she stepped into the rustic living room with its unmistakable masculine stamp. A chair and the burl coffee table had been pushed toward the center of the room. Frowning, she pointed.

"Small talk? That's how you want to start? I was trying to round up a ground squirrel. He must have climbed in the window I left open. He's out, finally."

Melaine could imagine Tanner chasing after a small, scurrying creature, trying to find a way to get it out of the house without panicking it. She concentrated on that instead of his hostile words. "Will you have to keep your window closed?" She sat uneasily at one end of the couch and stared into the black hole of the massive stone fireplace.

"No. I'd been working on the screen. I had it out. So . . ." He pushed the chair back into place and sat. "What are you going to tell me?"

"About what happened that morning."

"When your husband called and I made the mistake of picking up the phone. I was there, remember."

"Ex-husband," Melaine said automatically. Every window in Tanner's cabin had been left open. The incredibly clean scent of mountain air wafted around her, giving her strength. It took an incredible effort to focus on that distant past when she'd believed her life unbearable. "Tanner, I'd come to Nevada to get a divorce."

He opened his mouth, closed it, then opened it again. "Why didn't you tell me?"

Someday she'd have to tell him that he had an uncanny ability to zero in on the most painful questions. But if she did that now, she'd distract them from what had to be said. "I should have," she said softly, thinking how easy it had been for that ground squirrel to escape the confines of the house. He'd probably already forgotten his terrifying experience. Unfortunately, she couldn't shake off her past that easily. "I wanted to. But I hurt—"

"Hurt? Didn't you want the divorce?"

"The divorce, yes. The other, no."

"The other? Don't make me pull this out of you, Melaine."

He was right. Again. "I don't mean to. It's just that—" She glanced down at the couch. "I made a mistake. Probably the biggest mistake of my life."

"By not telling me about what's-his-name? I won't argue that."

"Chris. His name is Chris. No, that isn't it. I should never have married him."

"Beautiful. Then why did you?"

Melaine focused on Tanner's deep gray eyes and took her thoughts into the past, away from his hostility. "A thousand reasons. None of them the right one. Tanner, my parents were divorced when I was very young. I didn't have their marriage as an example of how two people are supposed to interact. Maybe that would have helped. I don't know. I . . . I was in college, not sure what I wanted to do with my life. Chris came along. He was handsome, moody, mysterious."

"And you fell in love with that?"

Love? Melaine wasn't sure she knew the meaning of the word where a man was concerned. "It's so hard to explain. I'm not sure I can. But all around me, people were pairing up. I wanted someone to care about the decisions I was trying to make. Someone to talk to. To—to go through life with. I thought Chris could be that one."

Melaine expected Tanner to say something, but he remained silent. Still.

Her eyes now drawn to his strong fingers draped over the edge of the chair arm, Melaine went on. "Those moody and mysterious qualities? I thought that meant he was one of those wounded men waiting for the right woman to free him from the past. Don't laugh. I was naive, so naive when it came to relationships."

"I'm not laughing."

No. He wasn't. "Chris and I were married for three years. In that time I learned that what I took for depth of emotion wasn't emotion at all. He was quiet because he didn't have much to say, I think. What he had wasn't enough for me." Melaine tried to face Tanner, but she felt moisture in her eyes. She couldn't let him see that. "I'm not the first woman to make a mistake about a man. But it was the first time I'd reached out to someone else like that. I didn't know how to handle the way it turned out."

Tanner leaned forward, his weight making the chair squeak. Startled, Melaine looked up. She half expected to see ridicule in his eyes. Instead she found silent, wary waiting. "It took you three years to decide you weren't right for each other?"

Melaine shook her head, comforted by the feel of her hair sliding over her jawline. "I went into marriage so naive, Tanner. I didn't stay that way long."

"Three years."

Yes. Three years. "That morning in the motel room, when you heard Chris on the line? It was easier to let you go than try to explain what I'd been going through."

"Wait a minute. You didn't love Chris when you left him. At least that's what you just told me, isn't it? What was so hard about getting a divorce then?"

Melaine drank in a deep breath of air, momentarily distracted by the clean taste in her lungs. Would she be able to do this if Tanner wasn't asking the right questions? Difficult questions. She didn't know. "Not the divorce. And not leaving Chris, although I couldn't help but feel as if I'd failed both of us."

"There's more, isn't there?"

"Yes. There's Amber."

"Amber? You have a child?"

Melaine pushed herself to her feet and walked quickly, silently, to the nearest window and looked up at the evergreens that surrounded Tanner's cabin. She felt both trapped by the massive trunks and freed by the graceful movement of blue-tinted tops swaying to the beat of the wind. "Not mine, although I'd give anything if she was. The thought of carrying . . . Chris was a widower. Amber was just a baby when he and I met."

"It was her you couldn't leave, wasn't it?"

"I was there when she spoke her first words, when she climbed on her first tricycle. I bought her clothes and held her at night when she was sick. I—she'd climb into my lap in the evening and we'd read the comics together. She's tall and athletic and beautiful. A mix of lacy little girl and tomboy." The tops of the trees blurred. Melaine blinked, but it didn't help. She reached for the window frame. She wondered if she could grip it tightly enough to keep from shaking. "She was four when we got divorced. Only four."

A heavy silence descended. Then in a horse whisper he said, "I wish I'd known."

Melaine heard a sound behind her, but couldn't tear herself free from the serenity of the trees. "I—couldn't speak her name without crying. I'm sorry I didn't tell you. But I knew if I tried, I'd end up—" She waved her hand. "It wasn't your problem. I didn't know how—"

She felt strength on her flesh. Tanner stood behind her, his fingers spread over her shoulders. She was careful not to lean into him; to do so was dangerous. Still, she couldn't make herself draw away. "How do you feel now?" he asked, the hard edge gone from his voice.

How? "There's no easy answer. I've been through so many emotions."

"Tell me about them?"

She couldn't do that, at least not all at once and not with him this close. "I, ah, I graduated from college with a degree in nursing. Being around Amber had a great deal to do with my decision. She had frequent ear infections. In the end she had to have surgery. We spent so much time with doctors and hospitals before the problem was corrected. I didn't want her going through that, of course. But those nurses—the ones who cared—they made a difference for Amber. I saw that and realized nursing was something I could do that would touch people's lives. Does that make sense?"

"Yes. It does."

Guided by his now-gentled tone, Melaine found the courage to say the rest. "Chris didn't understand what nursing meant to me. Maybe, maybe I didn't express myself in a way he could comprehend."

"I don't think that's it."

Despite her resolve not to risk any more than she already had, Melaine turned around. Tanner dropped his hands from her shoulder, but that didn't take away the imprint he'd made on her flesh. "What do you mean?" she asked.

"Melaine, in a few words you've made it possible for me to see what nursing means to you. If Chris couldn't do the same while living with you, then nothing you could say would possibly change that."

He was right. She had already known that. "No. It wouldn't," she said softly. "I think I just didn't want to admit that."

"Why not? You don't love him."

Love? Did she have any idea what it meant to love a man? "He's Amber's father. Admitting he wasn't interested in understanding how I felt about my career wasn't easy to face. It still isn't."

"Why should you care?"

"Why?" Although she wanted to push away from Tanner, she willed herself to lean against the window and go on facing him. "Because he's Amber's father. Because he can't see what's going on inside me. He's the same way with his daughter."

"What do you mean?"

"He . . . How do I explain this? Tanner, when Amber had earaches, Chris talked to the doctors. They told him about the corrective measure that was available as soon as she was old enough. After that, all he cared about was that we had the necessary medication in the house. It never occurred to him that she might need to be held and comforted because she was too young to grasp the idea that someday it would all be over."

A puzzled frown altered Tanner's features. Hopeful that he could understand what she was saying, Melaine went on. "I tried to be everything for Amber. I wanted to be. She didn't have a mother. She turned to me, and I reached for her. I believe I was instrumental in her turning out as self-confident as she is. But inside I was shriveling up."

"Shriveling? Why?"

"I don't . . . I said Chris didn't respect my career. I tried to convince myself that it didn't matter. After all, I didn't understand enough about his job. He designed a line of skis and now markets them throughout the United States. What he went through getting the business off the ground, well, it's something I'd never encountered before so I didn't know what it entailed. He never said much about it, and after a while I stopped asking." Melaine paused, wondering if Tanner could possibly care about what she was saying. But she'd said so much already that she didn't know how to stop. "His business means everything to him. It's his one passion in life. I thought I could make him understand that nursing was the same with me, but I couldn't.''

Tanner took a backward step and then, slowly, returned to his chair. Melaine followed suit, unable as before, to make herself relax. "He put down my career in front of Amber. He said I dress up in white and clean bed pans and say 'Yes, sir' to doctors. I told him that wasn't true. When that happened, for the first time in our marriage I yelled at Chris."

"The first time?"

Melaine couldn't quite meet Tanner's eyes. This was the hardest part to admit. "So much was building up inside me during those days. I resented being dismissed. It hurt because Chris had no idea what was going on inside me. And when I blew up that time, I knew I wouldn't be able to keep the lid on the volcano inside me any longer. I've never forgotten the look on Amber's face when it happened. The two most important people in her life were fighting. The woman she considered her mother had turned into a shrew. She didn't know how to handle it."

Feeling exhausted by what she'd just revealed, Melaine retreated into silence. She didn't know if Tanner had any idea what that time in her life had been like and how much her pain had influenced her decision to let him walk out of that hotel room. Leaving Amber a few days earlier had torn her into shreds. Bidding a silent farewell to a magical night with a stranger had been the only way she could survive back then.

Tanner ran a hand across the back of his neck. "Where is she now?"

"In Bishop," Melaine said, surprised by the turn the conversation had taken. "She and Chris moved there almost a year ago."

"And that's why you're here. So you can be near her."

"I have to." Hearing the strain in her voice, Melaine willed herself to be calm. "I'm the only mother she's ever known."

"And Chris doesn't mind his ex-wife remaining in touch with his daughter?"

Once that had been the subject of more arguments than Melaine wanted to think about. But, because a precious little girl was involved, she hadn't given up. "He knows I can't stop loving her. And Amber loves me. Having me help guide her toward adulthood, well, that frees him."

Tanner leaned back. They'd been talking long enough that it had begun to cool off outside. He should get up and close the windows, give her a clue that it was time for her to leave. He hadn't wanted to hear this. He hadn't wanted her to say something that would force him to react with concern and compassion. She'd touched him once. Once was more than enough.

Only, her midnight eyes told him that the argument he'd been carrying on with himself was far from over.

"I love the idea of running the clinic," she said. "Don't think I don't. It's the perfect job for me."

"But if she was somewhere else, you wouldn't be here, would you?"

"No. I probably wouldn't."

Tanner tensed his thigh muscles and then released them slowly. She hadn't changed. Not enough. She still wore her rich chestnut hair loose and long. Her thick lashes served as a sheltering frame for dark eyes filled with the lessons of life. Although she wore a loose sweatshirt and jeans, her woman's body beneath the layer of fabric reminded him of that night when she'd given herself to him and he'd lost himself in a stranger. "I don't know what I'm suppose to do with what you've told me," he said, unnerved by how hard he had to work at keeping his voice neutral. "At least I now have a pretty good idea what you were going through back then. But it's in the past."

"The past?"

Damn her hurting eyes. How could he pretend they

didn't exist? "Look, I've been married, too. I know how hard it is to put an end to it."

"You were? You do?"

Despite the way she stumbled over the word, Tanner didn't feel like laughing. "Yeah. It was one of those things college students do. Spring. Romance everywhere you turn. Friends getting married or moving in with someone. Thinking I'd found someone to spend the rest of my life with. It lasted less than a year."

"It took me longer."

"You had complications. Fortunately, Carla and I didn't have a child. A no-fault divorce is easy to get out of."

"Is it?"

She was right. Easy wasn't a word he could ever associate with divorce. Even now he had regrets, not that he and Carla were no longer married, but that he hadn't been what she needed. "I think . . ." Once again he ran his hand over the back of his neck, unable to remember what he'd done to make it feel so stiff. "You and I let Lake Tahoe and a summer sun and long nights come between us and everything we should have learned from our marriages. Fortunately, we bailed out before we got in too deep."

"Yes. We did."

The slow way Melaine spoke made him wonder if she really agreed with what he'd said. Still, he chose to take her words at face value. "Look, I was about to fix myself something for dinner. I don't mean to rush this, but I've got a meeting tonight."

"Oh." Melaine glanced down, as if not sure how to get to her feet. "I'm sorry. Of course. I just—" She stood and walked over to him, her hand stretched out tentatively. "You're right. We forgot certain lessons we should have known. That's all it was. It won't happen again."

"No. It won't." He stood and enveloped her hand in his, thinking, not about a conciliatory handshake, but how soft and warm and small her fingers felt in his. "I just wish I'd known what you'd been going through. I wouldn't have reacted the way I did."

Melaine pulled her hand free. "You wouldn't have broken the receiver?"

"I did that? I don't remember."

Melaine nodded and took a step toward the door. "I don't blame you."

"Water under the bridge. That's what my mother always said. That and something about crying over spilled milk. I'm glad we cleared that up."

"I'm glad you're glad."

This was insane. They were two mature professionals. Certainly they could carry on a conversation. Only, when he looked down at her, Tanner thought again of hot limbs clutching him in the night. Burying himself in her. Never wanting anything except to be a part of her.

Damning himself for the chance he was taking, Tanner touched her forearm. "It's none of my business; I know that. But your coming here so you can be near the girl—I think you've made a mistake."

"A mistake?"

"This Chris. He's Amber's parent. You don't have any legal claim to her, do you?"

"No." Melaine blinked. "But he said I could always be part of her life."

"Just like he said he'd always love, honor, and cherish you?"

Although he no longer touched her, Tanner sensed when Melaine drew her fingers into a tight fist. He'd hit her with a low but, he believed, necessary blow. "What are you saying?" she asked, her lips barely moving.

"That he might remarry. That he might decide one day that he wants to be the only influence in his daughter's life. What happens to you then?"

Pain creased Melaine's face so quickly and deeply that Tanner had to fight to keep from trying to shelter her against what his words had inflicted. "I can't think about that."

"It's reality, Melaine. You can't hide from reality."

"Don't. Don't tell me how to live."

Tanner stepped back, the gesture designed to let her know she was free to leave. "I won't. After all, it's not as if I'm part of your life."

"No." As she'd done before, Melaine spoke through lips that barely moved. "You aren't. What happened between us—it wasn't real."

No, Tanner thought as he watched Melaine walk from his place to her Jeep. Their one night together had nothing to do with reality.

Just as the way she'd chosen to live had nothing to do with him.

FIVE

Overloaded. Gun emplacements. Moguls. Snow fracture.

The words that tumbled so easily from Tanner and the other ski patrol members lips tangled in Melaine's mind, as if she needed reminding that their world was a new one to her. Yes, she could ski. She owned two ski outfits and her boots and skis were the latest in technology.

But she'd never ventured off groomed and well-marked runs while those she'd be working with were at home in a world she could barely imagine.

Tanner understood that.

"It's not the same as being there in the winter," he told her after the next night's EMT session. "The country changes so much that there's not much comparison. But you should know where we are when an emergency arises. The lay of the land, prevailing wind currents, any particular problems in getting an injured skier down to you—it'd be a lot easier if I don't have to stop what I'm doing to fill you in on the details."

Melaine agreed. The only thing she couldn't give her wholehearted approval to was Tanner's suggestion that she join him when he went to work the next morning. They'd be together all day, most of the time alone. And despite what they'd both said about putting the past behind them, she wasn't sure how well she'd be able to live up to her words.

Not as long as he insisted on wearing taut blue jeans and a limp T-shirt pulled over his broad chest. "Are you sure you want to do this?" she asked. "If you'd rather not—"

"What I do or don't want isn't the issue, Melaine. We have to work together."

"I know." She sighed. "It's just—"

"It's just that we're more than two people with a mountain in common. But right now . . ." He turned and faced her. "That mountain is the only thing that matters."

He'd changed from the frayed shirt, and this pair of jeans hadn't seen as many washings, but when she saw him the next day, Melaine still reacted. His physique told her he respected and took care of his body. The way he handled himself challenged her to deny his presence.

"You're on time," Tanner said when she joined him in the parking lot around Hut 2 a little before 7 A.M.

"Occupational hazard," she explained as she shrugged into the lightweight backpack he'd suggested she carry her lunch in. "I've worked every shift there is. I learned a long time ago to be flexible."

"That's good. This isn't going to be an eight-to-five job, not that I have to tell you that." Tanner slipped into his own backpack, flexing his muscles as he worked the straps into place. Melaine concentrated on the feel of her footwear. At least she tried to. "It's a lot different from a hospital setting, isn't it?" he continued. "What'd you do there? Did you have a specialty?"

As Tanner led the way up the trail that would take them to runs with names like Hangman's Hollow and Wipe Out, Melaine explained that she'd spent the majority of her time working in emergency but also had experience in surgery and orthopedics. Because he seldom turned back toward her, it was impossible to gauge his reaction to what she said about spending Friday and Saturday nights in a big city emergency room or weeks working to get accident victims out of bed and back on their feet. Melaine didn't try to downplay her emotional reaction to her career.

Chris hadn't been interested, and except for other nurses, she'd seldom had anyone to talk to.

When the increased elevation forced her to concentrate more on breathing and less on talking, Tanner explained that they could have taken one of the trams up, but he wanted to get a close-up look at the stability of the rocks around them. "You'll get used to the thinner air," he said. "But it's going to take a little time. Your legs aren't getting tired?"

They weren't because Melaine was used to spending her day on her feet. Still, she knew her muscles would be a little stiff in the morning. She also knew she wouldn't tell Tanner that. Instead, she asked him to explain why he was interested in rock stability. His comment about skier safety highlighted what she already knew; Tanner took his job just as seriously as she did hers.

She wondered if he'd come to that same conclusion, and if he had, whether it mattered to him.

Melaine leaned forward at the waist, pushing onward. Occasionally she glanced around at the wild and magnificent surroundings, but most of the time she concentrated on keeping her footing. And watching the rhythmic tightening of Tanner's leg muscles.

He was taking her into the wilderness. Away from civilization. He was Tarzan, she a trusting Jane. Only, she wasn't Jane any more than he was a savage ape man.

"There." Tanner stepped to one side, pointing upward. "I love seeing him."

Melaine followed the line of Tanner's strong arm. Soaring above the mountain, she spotted an eagle. The free and magnificent creature glided downward for several hundred feet before arching upward again. Melaine held her breath, wondering what it would feel like to capture the wind and ride it into tomorrow.

"That's why I couldn't stay in Sacramento," she whispered, awe altering her voice. "I'd never see an eagle in the city."

"I thought you came here because of Amber."

Melaine didn't shy away from his comment. "I don't expect you to understand." She took a deep breath, wishing her lungs would acclimate to the high altitude. "But if you met her—"

"I have two nieces. I know how delightful a child can be."

Delightful. Melaine turned the word around in her mind, but it didn't come close to what she felt for Amber. "It isn't the same thing. Your nieces, have they ever fallen asleep in your arms? Did you watch them grow from babies to girls? Did . . ." She stopped. She couldn't tell Tanner how much she'd wanted to hear Amber call her "Mother" and how deeply it had hurt when Chris wouldn't allow that.

Tanner was standing a little above her on the trail. He looked down, his eyes hooded against the summertime sun. "No. I didn't. But even if I had, I wouldn't have tried to take their father's place."

"That's because your nieces have a father. Chris isn't . . . Oh, Tanner, don't. I don't want to argue with you about this."

"I'm not arguing, Melaine. I'm simply saying that you're molding your life around a girl who isn't yours. It could end in heartache."

Heartache. Melaine knew all about the word. Hadn't it been her constant companion while she waited for the divorce to become final? If she hadn't been overwhelmed by the fear that she might never see Amber again, she wouldn't have sought escape in Tanner's arms. Certainly not.

Thank God that horrible time was behind her. If nothing

else, Chris understood that having his daughter and ex-wife remain part of each other's lives worked to his advantage. Amber needed a mother figure; Melaine was more than willing to provide that. As long as things continued the way they were, Melaine didn't try to rock the boat. She knew how futile that could be.

Having Tanner reappear in her life was a complication she hadn't anticipated, but they were two rational, reasoning human beings. They'd maintain a professional relationship.

Grunting, Tanner struck out again. Melaine fell into line behind him, but she couldn't dismiss what he'd just said. "It isn't your concern," she said to his back. "What Chris, Amber, and I work out is between the three of us."

Several heartbeats passed before Tanner, his voice tempered by the wind, agreed.

They ate lunch while sitting on a boulder nearly eleven thousand feet above sea level. From where they were, it was nearly impossible to make out the narrow roads that tried to tame the mountain, but Tanner pointed out where various landmarks were located. Fortified by the two summers she'd spent here, Melaine was able to keep up with his descriptions. She was fascinated by what he told her of helicopters capable of bringing expert skiers to remote areas, sleigh rides, snowmobile rentals, giant slalom races, the hot springs east of the airport.

By late afternoon, when she'd covered more country on foot than she dreamed possible and been awed by more spectacular views than she'd seen in her entire life, the hot springs were foremost in her mind.

"I went there a few times when I worked here, but those are the ones that have been developed. You said there are some that are pretty remote?" she asked, hoping to keep her question casual. She'd been wrong; she wouldn't have to wait until morning to feel the stress on her leg muscles. "Who goes there?"

"Employees mostly. I get there about once a week. If you remember, the smell isn't the best. The gas vents, you know. But if I've been pushing all day and my legs are tired—"

Melaine nodded, willing herself to match Tanner's pace. If this was his way of testing her competence, she was determined to pass the test, even if it meant crawling around on hands and knees tomorrow. Still, the idea of hot water swirling over her made her sigh with anticipation. As soon as they got back, she'd call Carol for directions.

"Would you like to go?"

"What?" Melaine pulled her attention back to where they were, or more specifically, the long climb back down off the mountain.

"To the hot springs. It's better than any salve for aching muscles. I'll take you there, if you want."

Did she? Keeping their conversation impersonal had taken all her attention today. She'd succeeded because there'd been a myriad of practical matters for them to discuss. But tonight they might put work behind them.

"You don't have to do that," she told him. "You must have more important things to do."

"No. Not really. I haven't been over there since before the new patrol members signed on. The truth? I've done twice as much walking today as I usually do."

Now he tells me, Melaine thought as she caught her fingers in a fist to keep from pounding him on the back. Still, she wasn't angry so much as puzzled by why he'd subjected both of them to this day-long climb. Did he really need to check the terrain this closely or, for reasons that escaped her, had he used the day as some kind of test? Of her? Of himself?

Of what might happen while they were together?

Well, nothing had. And it wouldn't.

* * *

Three hours later Melaine wasn't so sure. Somehow she'd managed to keep her feet under her while they scrambled and slipped down off the mountain. She'd sat on her side of the truck while Tanner drove back to the parking lot where she'd left the Jeep Bert loaned her and then forced her stiff and aching legs out of the truck's high cab. She'd willed herself not to groan, but when Tanner pointed out that they'd better run home for bathing suits first, she almost said no. If she spotted her bed, she'd probably fall on it facefirst. Still, there was no way she'd go to the springs with Tanner without the proper attire.

That reassurance lasted until they reached their destination, and she faced a couple of facts. One, they had the remote, rocky springs to themselves. Two, Tanner had removed his boots and was reaching for the fastening on his jeans. Although the sun had set, it wasn't yet dark. She'd be able to see Tanner, nearly all of him.

So?

So.

With a speed which made her wonder if he had the same thoughts, Tanner peeled off his jeans and shirt and stepped quickly into the waist-deep water. He wore a plain blue suit; still, her mind registered the way his dark hair trailed down his belly. She'd touched him there. She knew the feel of the thick, yet silken strands. His torso disappeared as he found something to sit on. Then, slowly, his legs floated upward, and he bent his head backward, sighing. "Wonderful. Absolutely wonderful."

He was waiting for her. If he could strip down to his suit that easily, she could. . . . Melaine struggled out of her shoes. She peeled off her socks, smiling a little at the marks left behind by the cotton ribbing. Her fingers felt awkward as she unfastened her own jeans and drew them over her hips.

He was watching. She felt his eyes on her but didn't feel brave enough to meet his gaze. She'd gained some ten pounds since that night in Nevada, but she'd lost a lot of weight during those final months while she struggled with the end of her marriage. Would he remember what she looked like back then?

What did it matter?

Pretending a casualness she was far from feeling, Melaine unbuttoned her cotton blouse and pulled it off her shoulders. She'd chosen a green one-piece suit with broad straps designed for swimming and not eye appeal. Still, it didn't leave enough to the imagination. She stepped into the hot, welcoming water, dropping the blouse on top of her jeans. It took her longer to find a place to sit than it had Tanner, and for the better of a minute, she stood with water caressing her hips.

What did it matter?

"How does that feel?" Tanner asked after she'd settled herself on a less-than-flat rock. "It's a little hot at first, but after a minute—"

Melaine barely heard what he was saying. Her unease around him had momentarily evaporated as heated, bubbling water eased her aching muscles. Tanner was right. The water was hot. It felt wonderful.

"I think I've died and gone to heaven." She sighed. "I'd forgotten how incredible hot springs can feel."

"As long as you don't breathe too deeply, it's quite an experience. Do you remember the smell?"

Melaine tried to give Tanner's question serious consideration, but the pines that surrounded them cut out most of what was left of the day. Other than Tanner's voice, the only other thing she could hear was the muted bubbling coming from the underwater springs. She'd been a different person when she first experienced this heat and aroma. Back then she'd known much less about life, dreams, the twists and turns of living.

Leaning forward as if that would shelter her from the male impact a few feet away, Melaine struggled to keep the conversation going. She said something about the commercialization of Mammoth over the years, but when he didn't press for a detailed explanation, she soon stopped.

It wasn't possible. It wasn't supposed to happen. What had passed between her and Tanner in that Nevada hotel had been nothing more than the insanity she'd been living during that time in her life. When, long after he'd walked out on her, his image returned, she had pushed it back down. If there was one thing she knew, it was that she didn't believe in love at first sight and maybe, for her, never. There was only one word for what she and Tanner had experienced.

Lust.

With the maturity that life had brought her, Melaine was able to look at the word, the experience dispassionately. Yes, she'd lost herself in Tanner's arms and forgotten what she knew and believed about herself. She'd buried herself in him, become a woman interested in nothing except the night. The forgetting of everything in a few hours of lovemaking.

Well, that woman had been buried by the return to sanity. Melaine never expected her to surface again. Never wanted her to.

So—why was it so hard to keep her distance from Tanner? Why, even now, did she want to feel his legs drifting over to hers? Why did the thought of his hands on her body heat her in a way the bubbling, pulsing springs never could?

Melaine sucked in sulphur-smelling air and willed herself to look, not at Tanner but out at the shadows that surrounded the evergreens and isolated them from the world.

"Bert told me Carol's pregnant."

Tanner's voiced pulled her, a little, out of her thoughts. "Yes," she replied, her voice not much more than a whisper.

"And that you're going to take care of her. She's all right, isn't she?"

"Fine. Of course I wouldn't be doing the actual delivery, and if there are any problems, I'll send her to a doctor. But she takes wonderful care of herself." The undulating pressure guided her legs closer to Tanner. Or maybe the truth was, she was allowing herself to be drawn toward him.

"That's good." Tanner repositioned himself on his perch, the gesture erasing a few of the inches which separated them. "She's a good woman."

"Yes." Melaine's toe brushed something. Tanner's leg? "She is."

"Bert's excited. A little scared, but a lot excited."

"Is he?" Yes. It had to be Tanner's leg. Otherwise an electric current wouldn't have surged through her.

"It's—it's something he hadn't really thought about. Boy, girl, he doesn't care as long as it's healthy."

"That's—what most people say."

"Do they?"

"Most of them," Melaine repeated. She sought through her mind for something else to say, but no words managed the journey from her brain to her mouth. It had become so dark that she wasn't sure whether Tanner was looking at her or not. She thought so; she hoped so even while she hoped he had better things to do than concentrate on her.

What insanity had made her think she might be immune around him? Nothing more had happened than a brushing of her toe against his calf and yet her body hummed with need. She wanted to tell him everything that had happened to her since their other time together. She'd let him know about the lonely but necessary nights spent alone, the drive to bury herself in her work, the dreams.

What would he think of her dreams?

Would he know that he was the man she reached for when substance became shadow and reality slid into desire?

When she felt the whisper of his thigh a hand's breath

from hers, Melaine fought the fire inside and struggled for words. Any words. "You—you and Bert are good friends?"

"What? Bert? Yes."

"That's good." Oh God, she needed more than that tantalizing whisper. "Carol belongs here. She's competent, sure. She loves—what she does."

"Bert's—the same way. Not enough people find the person who's right for them."

Could you ever be right for me?

Frightened by the question and how little control she had over its existence, Melaine stared first out at the inky expanse that was the hot springs and then up at the sky, impatient for the emergence of the first star, anything to fasten her mind on. "No. Not many do."

"Like your parents," Tanner whispered. His words rolled softly toward her, aided by the wind. "Their getting divorced must have been hard on you."

"I guess. I was so young."

Silence. Once again silence. There was no way she could be sure, but the sense that Tanner was looking at her was so strong that she didn't try to deny it. Was he thinking about her upbringing? It seemed incredible that he was capable of any rational thought when she remained a willing, frightened prisoner to erotic musings.

When she wanted nothing except the feel of his hands on her warm, wet body.

This time, when flesh brushed against flesh, Melaine didn't draw back. Touching him, being touched in return either by accident or design, was like getting back in a car after an accident. She could do it. Certainly the feel of his calf brushing over her shinbone was nothing compared to the thousands of bodies she'd prodded and massaged and explored over the course of her career.

Certainly his flesh, his warm flesh was no different than—

He'd known everything she needed during that night

three years ago. She hadn't had the power of speech, hadn't understood what primitive drive guided her to his arms. But he'd sensed her crying, lonely need.

He'd turned need into fire.

And they'd held each other and dove into the inferno.

And tonight flesh against flesh threatened to become flint and steel.

"Melaine?"

"What?"

"I think—"

"Yes." *Speak. Say the necessary words.* "It's time to leave."

SIX

During the next five days, Melaine saw Tanner twice. Once their vehicles passed on the narrow road around Lake Mary. The second time he dropped by with a forest ranger in tow. He stayed just long enough to introduce Melaine to the ranger and show the middle-aged man around the clinic.

Melaine spent her days unpacking and stocking supplies, learning more than she ever thought she'd have to about the area's communication system, acting as Bert's assistant on several projects, and sampling Carol's basic but welcome cooking. Each night either she called Amber or Amber made a collect call to her. Her phone bill would rival the national debt, but then that was nothing new.

She no longer felt overwhelmed by the job she'd taken on. So far her patients consisted of fishermen who'd hooked themselves instead of fish, hikers with twisted ankles, sunburned vacationers who didn't respect the power of high mountain sunshine.

Finally she felt she could take off long enough to go see Amber. The trip would have to be a quick one because Bert and Carol were expecting her at an end of the summer party on Saturday.

"I don't know who else to ask," she told Tanner when

she called him that evening. "I was hoping one of the members of your ski patrol could keep an eye on the clinic for a day. I'd be back before evening."

"You're going to see Amber?"

Ignoring what she interpreted as disapproval in Tanner's voice, Melaine explained that Amber was anxious to spend time with her before school began. "I've already been here over a week. She doesn't understand the work involved in opening a new clinic. I'm hoping she can spend a lot of her weekends here, but right now, well, it's easier for me to run down there than try to arrange for her to come here. She's a little anxious about starting in a new school. I thought, if we had time to really talk, it would help."

Tanner suggested Melaine call Red. The young patrol member was nursing a large blister on his heel and wouldn't be able to join the others on the mountain until it healed. "You're going to need a reliable backup all right. Otherwise, you're never going to get any time off. Only, I hope you're planning to do more with your life than going to see Amber."

Melaine stiffened. For the past five days her thoughts of Tanner had revolved around those unsettling and yet heady moments they'd spent at the hot springs. She'd managed to half convince herself that the only thing she had to deal with where he was concerned was the lingering and irrational physical attraction.

He'd just reminded her of what else remained unresolved between them.

"You still don't understand, do you?" she asked. "This isn't something I'm doing out of duty. There's nothing I want more than to spend time with her."

"Even if it means putting your own life on hold? . . . I'm sorry, Melaine. It's none of my business."

"No. It isn't."

"Right. Only, I can see you getting your heart broken

again if something happens in Chris's life. I got a glimpse of what you went through before, remember."

Melaine didn't have to listen to this. Briefly, unemotionally, she reminded him that, no, it *wasn't* his life. She thanked him for suggesting Red as her backup and then hung up. She'd been going to tell him about the chipmunk that had taken up residence at the rear of the clinic. She'd wanted him to know that the pictures she'd taken for Bert had been developed, and they were awe-inspiring. Now neither of those things mattered.

Tanner didn't understand. He couldn't possibly.

Amber had grown, most of the length going into her long legs. She reminded Melaine of a young horse who hadn't quite figured out how to handle its sudden ability to race the wind. None of Amber's clothes from last year fit. Chris had bought several outfits, but she wanted to try them on in front of Melaine to make sure no one at school would laugh. She'd decided she'd look good in bangs and would Melaine please cut them for her since she didn't trust anyone else to do it right. Melaine was fascinated by the change from total tomboy to budding girl; she was also saddened by thoughts of how much of the journey she'd missed recently.

"He never comes home for lunch," Amber explained when Melaine asked if Chris would be joining them. "Sometimes Mrs. McKinsey takes me into the shop, but usually Daddy's so busy he doesn't have time to eat. He's on the phone *all* the time."

Melaine turned from her study of Amber's room with its posters of Disney characters, baseball heroes, and young rock stars against a backdrop of rumpled yellow bedspread and a four-foot high panda—Melaine's gift on her sixth birthday. "He works a lot of hours?" she asked. Unconsciously, she touched the photograph of her that Amber kept on her nightstand.

"A lot. Everyone loves Daddy's skis, but he doesn't

trust anyone else to make them right. That's what he says. If he's going to be rich, he has to make sure nothing goes wrong."

What about time with his daughter? Melaine thought but didn't voice her misgivings. She'd battled that question a thousand times; the answer never changed. Seizing the opportunity to be with Amber, she asked to be taken on a tour of the rest of the large, nearly new house, and then suggested they drive over to the elementary school. Amber couldn't see any reason to get out and take a look at the playground, but Melaine insisted. After a little prompting on Melaine's part, they tried out the swings and slide. Finally Amber demonstrated her agility on a free-form structure made from thick rope and unfinished wood. "You're going to leave the rest of the girls in your dust. You know that, don't you?" Melaine said. "They'll be standing around giggling and you'll be playing baseball with the boys."

"Do you think so?"

"I know so." Melaine hugged her to her. "You show those boys that you can run the bases with the best of the them, and you'll be very popular."

"I don't care about that. I just want some friends."

Melaine leaned forward so she could look Amber in the eye. "You said something about a boy in your neighborhood. I thought he was your friend."

"He is." A little of the hesitancy faded from Amber's eyes. "He says we're going to have a man teacher some of the time. I met the principal. His daughter goes to the same day care I do."

"Didn't you say there are several kids in day care your age? Maybe they'll all be in your class."

"Maybe. The principal's girl is nice. But shy. I wonder why?"

"Maybe it's hard being the principal's daughter. I wouldn't be at all surprised if she'd like a friend. She just doesn't know how to get started."

"Do you think so?" Amber asked as Melaine guided her back to her car. Melaine replied that she wouldn't be at all surprised. In fact, maybe Amber could get her phone number and call her. Buoyed by that thought, Amber began talking enthusiastically about what she'd wear the first day. With Amber now in a talkative mood, they spent a couple of hours exploring Bishop before Melaine drove them to the new building which housed Powder and Ice Skies. Amber nodded and said hello to the receptionist. She introduced Melaine as her "very best friend in the whole world." Then, in a very mature, very proper voice, Amber asked if she could see her father. Melaine met the receptionist's eyes. The other woman's look echoed what Melaine believed; a child shouldn't have to ask if her father had time for her.

Despite her lingering depression over that inescapable fact, Melaine was impressed by what she saw. Not only was the building much larger than she expected, but it had been constructed with an eye to blending in with the central California landscape. She doubted that the stone and natural wood design had been Chris's idea. Unless he'd changed radically since their divorce, aesthetics weren't a priority with him. He must have hired an architect, who saw buildings as an art form, and the architect must have convinced Chris that this particular design would benefit business.

"It's incredible," Melaine told Chris when they finally located him in his office behind the showroom. She shook his hand, noting that the calluses forged by his hands-on approach to business had, if anything, become tougher. "You've what, doubled your business since—"

"Since the divorce." Chris acknowledged his daughter's presence, but didn't stop his study of whatever was on his computer screen long enough to hug her. "More than doubled. Yeah. I'm off the ground all right. The problem is, I've already outgrown this place. Expansion's going to be a problem. I've gone public, you know. You wouldn't like to buy stock in the company, would you?"

Melaine wasn't sure that was a good idea, but because she was more interested in watching the interplay between father and daughter, she didn't bother to spell that out. After looking through a sales catalogue on his desk, Amber walked around so she could study the monitor. "We have computers at school. That's what Andy says."

"Andy?" Chris smoothed the edges of the catalogue.

"You know," Amber said, exasperation in her voice. "Andy Mina down the street. He's my boyfriend. Not a real boyfriend. But he's a boy and he's my friend."

Melaine smiled, remembering her years of trying to decide how boys fit or didn't fit in her life. She also noted that Chris had his fingers poised over his keyboard.

He'd aged. True, if anything he looked even more physically fit than he had when they were married, but there were new lines at the corners of his eyes and others angling his mouth downward. He'd lost some of his hair and the flesh on the back of his hand no longer had that hard, firm look. Knowing that she'd undergone the same aging process didn't bother Melaine. Her mind was on the sad and inescapable fact that nothing, not even a visit from his daughter and ex-wife, had distracted Chris from his work.

She asked a number of questions about what it was like living in Bishop, what Chris thought of Amber's day-care center, if he was pleased with the direction the business was taking. The only time he looked up from the computer was when he explained that, despite Bishop's relative isolation, he was able to fill East coast orders in less than a week.

"I was thinking . . ." Melaine began slowly, feeling her way. "It looks as if you're pretty busy right now, gearing up for winter. What if I took Amber back with me? She could stay until school starts."

"Hmm." Chris punched something into the computer, paused, then hit the delete button. "I don't see why not."

"Daddy." Melaine heard the sad note Amber's voice. "I can't."

"Why not?"

"Andy's birthday party. He asked me to come. He really wants me 'cause his mother said he had to invite some girls so there wouldn't be so much fighting. I said yes. I told you about it last night."

Chris blinked, glanced at Melaine, Amber, then returned his attention to the computer. "Did you? I guess I forgot. Well, why don't you and Melaine work it out. I don't care."

Melaine felt like screaming. Of course what he was doing was important. Close to thirty employees earned a livelihood from the business. However, his daughter's life was just as important. Pressing the point a little, Melaine explained that she wouldn't think of having Amber miss the party. A promise was a promise. Besides, this would be a way for Amber to meet a few more kids. Amber, a little of the sparkle gone from her eyes, asked if Melaine could come for her after Andy's party. But that would take them into next weekend, and Melaine had been at Mammoth long enough to know that her work would double on the weekend.

"I don't know what we're going to do, honey," she said. "Maybe we won't be able to work out anything before school starts."

"Really?" Amber moaned. "But that's so long."

"She could take the bus."

Melaine hadn't thought Chris had been paying attention to the conversation. It took her a moment to digest his comment. "A bus? You want Amber to come by bus?"

"Why not? I use the system. They can get skis to southern California in one day."

A pair of skis, even a hundred pairs of skis, was far different from an eight-year-old girl. "I would rather she didn't," Melaine said, as usual feeling her way when it came to Chris's authority over his daughter. "She's too young to be traveling alone."

"What? Look, I trust the system."

"You don't have to worry about someone kidnapping your skis," Melaine blurted. "Look, I know someone. He's a pilot. I think, if I worked out the details with him, he'd be willing to pick Amber up the next time he comes to Bishop."

Chris had no objection to that. And, as she suspected, Amber was wildly excited about the idea of flying in a small plane. In an attempt to take Amber past the disappointment of not being able to come to Mammoth right away, Melaine launched into a description of the deer Bert had shown her. Once again Amber's eyes took on a lively sparkle.

Chris hunched over his computer.

After a too long, too lonely drive back to Mammoth, Melaine tried to distract herself by returning to the clinic. She managed to grab Red as he was closing for the day and had him tell her about the day's business. Finally, though, there was nothing for her to do but go back to the A-frame which wouldn't have seemed so large and quiet if Amber had been there.

Working automatically, Melaine fixed herself a simple supper and then tried to settle down to watch TV. But even with it on, she was aware of the sharp contrast between the sound of Amber's laughter and the canned cackles plugged into the situation-comedy rerun.

That's what he doesn't understand, Melaine thought as she switched channels. There's nothing as precious, or as necessary, as a child's laughter.

She wasn't sure whether her message was designed for Chris or Tanner.

* * *

"No. Not a thing," Carol said when Melaine called to ask what she could contribute to the party. "We get the area restaurants to cater the affair and it's always held at Sierra Lodge so all I have to do is make sure everyone shows up. Throw on a little makeup and get in a mood to cut loose. Believe me, as soon as the snow starts falling, you won't have a moment to call your own."

Melaine really wasn't in the mood for an end of the summer bash, but Carol had a point. Now, before both snow and tourists descended, was the perfect time for the resort's residents to enjoy each other in relative calm.

Deciding on a soft yellow sweater and white slacks distracted Melaine from the question of whether Tanner would be there, and what they'd find to say to each other. Touching mascara to her lashes and light shadow to her lids gave her something to do other than miss Amber.

Finally, both needing and dreading the evening, Melaine drove over to the massive stone-and-timber lodge. As she stepped out, she was bombarded with the sound of a live rock band. The heavy beat of a drum, the power of an amplified guitar captured her senses.

Feeling alive and a little wild, Melaine walked up the stairs and into the lodge.

Tanner was already there. How she found him in the crush of bodies packed into the huge banquet room, she couldn't say. Maybe there wasn't a sensible or sane explanation. He simply was. She simply reacted.

For the first time, he wore something other than jeans and white T-shirt pressed to his body. The dark-blue turtleneck sweater and casual tan slacks reflected what half of the men then wore, and yet on Tanner, at least for her, the message went deeper.

Look. But don't touch. If that's possible.

He stood in the middle of a group of young, athletic men laughing over something that brought out hearty chuckles. Melaine stood, her ears somehow sorting his voice from the others. Then he turned and faced her. His eyes still sparkled; his mouth still lifted in the pure enjoyment of life. And yet—it was in his body, a subtle shifting and drawing inward as if he needed to protect himself from something.

From her?

Holding her own smile in place, Melaine weaved her way around the crowd of people toward him. She stuck out her hand, wondering what his reaction would be. When he engulfed her fingers with strength, she was struck by the difference between his hand and Chris's. Or maybe the difference was in her reaction.

"You've been busy," he said as a couple of his friends turned in their direction. "I understand you've been putting in a lot of overtime."

"No more than you have." Melaine didn't try to draw her hand free. It would happen when Tanner was ready to release her. In the meantime she'd react. And try to make sense of the reaction. "I don't see how you can do any more during the winter."

"If I've done my preparation right, I won't have to. Your trip to Bishop. How did it go?"

Because he'd released her, Melaine was able to answer. She concentrated on the neutral aspects of what had happened by telling Tanner about expansion to the elementary school, the location and design of Chris's business, how long the round trip had taken. He nodded and asked a couple of questions about Powder and Ice Skiis. His eyes never left hers.

Melaine hadn't been sure what they would talk about once the topic of Bishop was behind them. Fortunately, she didn't have to make that decision. Although she knew most of the men with Tanner, there were a couple of newcomers. They obviously felt no hesitation about introducing themselves to her and one, the owner of a group of cabins on Lake Mary, launched into a description of the work he'd been doing on the cabins' roofs. He wanted her to let him know if the A-frame roof leaked, and if it did, he would do the repairs for the cost of the labor. Melaine thanked him and told him she'd remember the offer.

Red placed a glass of wine in her hand. She tried to thank him, but the sound coming from the band made conversation difficult. As young members of the party commandeered the center of the room for spontaneous and enthusiastic dancing, Melaine allowed Tanner to draw her close to a wall. He said something about the fall colors, but because she caught only about half of what he was saying, she simply nodded a reply. He started to speak again, shrugged, then half turned from her and concentrated on the dancers.

After a few minutes, Carol grabbed her and hauled her into the huge industrial kitchen. She needed help finding room to refrigerate everything. Melaine tried to approach the subject of Bert flying Amber here, but Carol had too much on her mind to concentrate.

Melaine's thoughts returned to Tanner. Had he found someone to dance with? Would he care whether she returned to his side?

"Enough with this." Carol sighed and slammed the refrigerator door closed. "I want to dance while I can still get around." She grabbed Melaine's hand and hauled her back into the crowded room.

When Bert commandeered his wife with the statement that he was going to show the younger generation a step or two, Melaine stepped back to watch. Yet, despite herself, she soon turned toward where she'd last seen Tanner.

He was watching her.

And before the song was over, he'd started in her direction.

Fool. Tanner chided himself. *Fool.* If he had any semblance of sense, he'd leave her alone. If she had any idea what he'd been thinking about lately, she wouldn't blame her if she told him he'd lost his mind. Sitting out on his deck until well past dark, staring out across the lake, fantasizing about her doing the same thing—allowing his thoughts to become tangled in memories of a hot-blooded, silent woman surrendering her body to his in an impersonal hotel room—

Without speaking, Tanner touched his hand to Melaine's waist, indicating he wanted to dance. He was, he told himself, giving her every opportunity to turn him down. Certainly he'd understand.

Only, she was pacing her steps to his, allowing their shoulders to brush, looking up at him while they waited for the music to begin.

With a silent groan—or was it a sigh—he squared around to face her. The music, the beat, wasn't designed for cheek-to-cheek dancing. He had only a rudimentary understanding of what he was expected to do on the dance floor, but from what he'd observed, he didn't think that mattered. Modern dancing seemed to consist of random body movements, sensual or athletic, awkward or smooth, with a partner or without.

He had a partner.

Melaine threw her head back, tossing her hair away from her cheeks. After wincing at the crash of sound, she smiled, shrugged, and began a series of movements that stripped Tanner's mind of any awareness of what extended beyond her.

Lord, but she had a grace about her. That plus a softly curving body capable of meshing muscle and bone into perfect rhythm.

If Melaine had any hesitancy about what she was doing, it didn't show. She seemed to take her cues from the vibration of sound, the energy building around them—maybe even from the admiration he knew he couldn't keep from transmitting to her. Without drawing undue attention to herself, Melaine lost herself in the primitive sound. She pulled her shoulders back slightly, the gesture thrusting her breasts outward. She held her head aloft, her arms gliding through the air in sleek, sweeping movements that made him ache with the need to feel those arms on him.

Velvet strength.

One song seemed to end, but before he could be sure, another began. It started with the same hard, sensual rhythm and then gentled. Gentled *her*. With that totally absorbed smile still transforming her usually serious mouth, Melaine slid closer to him until their bodies were within a heartbeat of touching. Through layers of clothing, Tanner felt her heat. He breathed quickly, deeply, sucking in her perfume.

It went to his head. Flowed through his body.

Closer, closer, until they touched. Then, teasing as much as he was being teased, Tanner broke the contact. The heated glitter dancing in her eyes told him he'd made his point.

Tell me you don't feel it. Go on. Lie to both of us.

She didn't lie. She didn't speak.

The drummer picked up the beat. Melaine lifted her head again and her eyes glazed slightly. She parted her lips. Tanner tried not to notice; he failed. She seemed jointless now as if driven by nothing except the sound in the air, the sound pulsing through her.

Tanner felt himself being taken over by the same rhythm. He didn't try to fight. On some instinctive level he understood that he'd gone too far to pull back from the power the band had created. He'd felt that potency before, every time he committed to a downhill run. Knowing that his strength was nothing before that of a vast mountain, understanding that survival was possible only if he surrendered to that power had always filled him with excitement, fear, challenge.

He felt the challenge tonight. The fear. The excitement. Not because he'd allowed a wildly beating drum to control his heart's cadence but because a woman, this woman, shared the experience with him.

"God!"

Tanner focused. Melaine still hadn't closed her mouth. She breathed through flared nostrils, her cheeks flaming, the hair around her temple sweat-soaked.

"You like it?"

"I love it!" She smiled, her grin not quite civilized, not quite primitive. "Music. It's been so long."

"You're a good dancer."

"Am I? I have no idea what I'm doing. But it doesn't matter. It doesn't." Her lids slid down over her eyes, shutting Tanner off from her thoughts.

He longed to reach out and stop her retreat, but he was afraid to try. His own body, hot and damp and pulsing, recorded, not drum and guitar but the sensuality of a fast-breathing, fast-moving woman.

He wanted her. Just like that. No preliminaries, no reason, just wanted.

Knowing there was only one way of keeping the beast at bay, Tanner threw himself into the beat. From out of the corner of his eyes, he glimpsed Bert as the older man grasped his wife to him, a hearty laugh sluicing through other sounds. Red pounded into sight, a solidly built blonde matching him move for move. Couples, young, old, tentative and free-wheeling joined him and Melaine, and yet he was aware only of her.

Wanted only her.

Needed nothing but her.

Finally, when the quick expansion and contraction of his lungs threatened to take away his ability to concentrate, the band slammed the room into silence. For a couple of heartbeats, Tanner rode out the silence. Then laughter and loud, excited voices filled the void.

Melaine gripped his upper arm and pressed her forehead against his shoulder. "Thank heavens! I'm getting too old for this."

Old? Tanner felt anything but old.

"Tanner?"

He forced himself to focus. Melaine's face glistened.

She wiped her free arm over her forehead and smiled up at him, her mouth still parted in invitation.

But maybe it wasn't invitation after all.

"What?" he finally thought to ask.

"I need . . . it's so hot in here."

Hot? Oh yes, hot.

"Would you like to go outside?"

She did. While the band took a break, he and Melaine stood in front of the building. They weren't alone. Conversation revolved around recent weather reports, a rumor that gravel might be put down on the trail up to Panorama Dome, the temperature of the water at Twin Falls. His arm casually, oh so casually, around Melaine, Tanner contributed to the various topics. Slowly he regained control over his breathing and his flesh cooled. He felt the same reaction in her. She added little to the talk. Instead she let her arm trail lightly around his waist, laughed when he laughed, listened when he spoke. And smiled.

When Carol announced that the grub was ready, and it was every man for himself, Tanner guided Melaine back inside and encouraged her to try everything, including a few strange-looking dishes he avoided. After the meal was over, the band began again, and once more Tanner guided Melaine out onto the dance floor. If anyone else wanted to dance with her, that was too bad.

He needed this.

He wanted her to need it just as much.

The party began breaking up a little before midnight. Although he knew he should single out the resort owners to compliment them, Tanner convinced himself he could do that tomorrow.

Tonight was for walking Melaine through the night-quiet streets.

"I can smell it." Her hand nestled securely if not easily in Tanner's hand, Melaine matched his easy stride.

"What?"

"Winter. It's coming. There's something new in the air. The smell of snow."

Tanner looked down at her. "Just because we had a snow dance tonight doesn't mean it'll be here tomorrow."

He was right, of course, but Melaine didn't bother to agree. During the day, the streets were jammed with tourists intent on grabbing a piece of the last of summer. Now the stores were closed and the tourists had left. Thanks to the streetlights, she was able to focus on the architecture of various lodges, restaurants, and condominiums. The mix of naturally fading wood exteriors next to exacting replicas of Swedish villas somehow all blended together. Or maybe, given her mood, anything would have added to the mystique.

Why had she agreed to taking this short walk with him? Her legs and feet ached from the unaccustomed exertion. She'd barely get to bed in time to get up and begin a new day. And being alone with Tanner was neither wise nor sane. Still—

"Why did you come here?" she asked after a long silence that was both comfortable and alive with electricity. "You told me you liked working at Squaw Valley."

"I did. I'm still drawn to the place. But when I started hearing rumors that Mammoth and June were going to be under the same ownership, I sensed a new challenge. A way of stretching myself."

A way of putting certain locations and memories behind him? Melaine shook off the thought. Although she'd never quite freed herself from Tanner, she didn't believe his brief impact had guided the direction her life had taken. Maybe in one small way. Because she'd spent a night in his arms, she'd learned that, despite everything, she was truly alive.

"What about you?" he asked. "Was wanting to be close to Amber the only reason you came here?"

"No. I had those wonderful memories from my teenage years. Oh, I knew that things would have changed, that I wasn't the same girl I'd been when I worked here. But I knew what Mammoth had to offer in the way of quality of life. I was drawn to that."

"It didn't bother you, uprooting yourself? What about your family?"

Her family. Except for her sisters, who now had separate lives of their own, there wasn't anyone. "Tanner, except for Amber, I'm a pretty independent woman. There aren't that many ties in my life."

"I'm sorry."

"Are you?" she asked, puzzled. He still held her hand. They walked slowly, hips occasionally brushing as the narrow sidewalks kept them in close proximity.

"Yes," he said softly. "I know I told you about my parents. How close we are. I remember you didn't say much."

"No." Melaine drew out the word, feeling uneasy. Tonight, with the pure sensual experience of dancing still driving her, wasn't the time to tell him about her background. "I didn't. Tanner, you said you've been married. What was she like?"

Tanner glanced down, obviously surprised by her question. "Carla? A college student. We met while we were both in college."

"I know that. What was she like as a human being?"

Tanner slowed. Melaine thought he might draw away from her, but he continued walking, staring ahead.

"She loves to laugh. Life's a grand adventure to her. Anything new, anything she hasn't experienced, that's what draws her."

Were these the words of a man who'd put his marriage behind him? Melaine couldn't answer that. "And that's what you saw in her? Her adventurous nature."

"I think so. At least at first. I fell hard. We were inseparable. My friends told me I'd really gone off the deep end, but I didn't mind."

"No." The word came out a whisper. "I don't imagine you did."

Tanner glanced down at her, frowned, then again concentrated on the sidewalk. As Melaine continued to match her step to his, he told her about the girl who changed her major three times in a little over a year, who chafed for an entire summer because they couldn't afford to tour Europe. Carla worked part-time during the school year as a waitress, making an incredible amount of money in tips because the customers liked her outgoing nature. For a long time Tanner rode the wave of energy radiating from his young wife.

But in the end, love died. Or maybe reality stepped in and took its place. Tanner had finished college and was eager to get on with his life. He was focused; he wanted to work out of doors. He learned from forest rangers, ski patrol members, search-and-rescue crews, defining his own area of expertise. Carla remained in college, dabbling in philosophy, art, journalism, even chemistry. And she was happy as a waitress.

"We didn't have the same goals," Tanner finished. "I knew what I wanted out of life. She didn't. She wanted us to spend our evenings discussing the meaning of life with her free-thinking friends. I'd been working all day. I was tired. I wanted to go home, think about what needed to be done tomorrow, be alone with my wife."

Melaine bit down on her lower lip to keep from reacting to the words "my wife." "Your divorce? It was your idea?"

"Both of ours. We stay in touch. She hasn't remarried. I can't keep track of the men who've been in her life. I think she's beginning to realize she's out of step with what most people are doing, but that isn't my agenda. I can't be the one to guide her life. She taught me something, though." He glanced down at Melaine. "So did you. The only person I can be true to in this world is myself."

They'd turned back toward the lodge where they'd left

SNOW SOUNDS / 87

their vehicles. As the massive structure came into sight, Melaine squared her shoulders. She'd wanted this time alone with Tanner. With her body still humming from the music she'd absorbed, with her blood heated from Tanner's touch, she didn't want the evening to end.

And yet she did.

Because, like Tanner, she'd learned that only she could direct and live her life.

Only she knew what she needed.

SEVEN

Three days after the party, Melaine had just walked in the door when the phone rang. She picked up the receiver and sank into a chair. When she recognized Chris's voice, she straightened.

"Is anything wrong? Amber's all right?" she asked.

"Fine. Just fine. Look, what you said about wanting her to stay with you for a few days. Does that still go?"

"Of course," Melaine blurted. "You know how I feel about that."

"Right. Melaine, I've got a problem. Maybe you can help me out."

Melaine wasn't prepared to have Chris ask her for help. If there was one thing she knew about her ex-husband, it was that he believed in standing on his own two feet. Only, as he outlined his situation, she came to appreciate his dilemma. Business matters made it necessary for him to spend at least a week in Aspen. It simply wasn't practical to take Amber with him. He'd offered to pay his housekeeper extra to keep her, but Mrs. McKinsey's husband was due back in town and she didn't want to be tied down.

"I don't know what else to do. There simply aren't any

places around here where children can stay for that length of time."

That's right, Melaine thought. Unfortunately for Chris, children couldn't be boarded out like animals. Wisely she kept that to herself. Instead she concentrated on the logistics of getting Amber to Mammoth, concerned because the girl would miss several days of school. Chris didn't see that as a particular problem. Amber was a bright child; she'd be able to catch up.

That wasn't the point, Melaine thought once the conversation was over. Amber wouldn't be there during some of those vital early days when friendships were formed. Still, the thought of having Amber with her meant so much. She'd make sure Amber had the phone numbers of both Andy and the principal's daughter.

Because she'd spent the evening readying the spare bedroom, Melaine had to drag herself to work. Fortunately, she didn't have many patients and was able to concentrate on the meals she'd cook for Amber, the things she'd show her.

She was mentally picturing Amber's reaction to the mountain-stream picture she'd hung over Amber's bed when Tanner pulled into the parking lot. She glanced up, surprised and yet not surprised to see him. Even with Amber on her mind, she hadn't quite dismissed him and what he'd said about his determination to live his own life.

The words had been wise; she just wasn't sure how well she'd accepted them.

Late-afternoon sunlight followed Tanner inside, salting his jet hair with burnished highlights. For a moment, nothing existed for her except that. Then, shaking her head, she made herself concentrate on what he was saying.

"I thought you needed to know. Not that I really expect anything to come from it, but it's going to make some people uneasy." He ran his fingers over the back of his left hand, drawing Melaine's attention to a bruise there. "We've been getting a few rumbles. The quakes are barely registering on the Richter scale, but because the epicenter is close, a few rocks have been shaken loose."

Melaine perched herself on her desk, trying to keep her eyes on his. Only, he was back in jeans. A man built for jeans. "Is that how you got the bruise?"

Tanner glanced at his hand. "This? I don't remember where it came from. Occupational hazard. Bert built the clinic to earthquake specs so you don't have to worry about that. But as long as the earth's doing its little dance, we're going to have to stay on the alert."

Melaine understood that. She also wondered why Tanner had made a special trip here to tell her that. Could it be that, like her, he felt there'd been something unfinished about the other night? "I'll keep that in mind," she told him.

"I just wish . . ." He paused as a gust of wind blew in the open window, and she placed a book on some loose papers. "Winter. Just around the corner. I was thinking, I wish there was a better way of predicting quakes. If I knew when one was coming, I could get people off the slopes before anything happened."

"Tanner, that isn't your responsibility. This is California. Earthquakes are part of it."

"I guess." Tanner walked over and closed the door. He didn't speak until he'd leaned against the table she sat on. "It looks like you've got things pretty well organized here."

Melaine nodded, pleased that he'd noticed. "I think so. It's a good thing because I'm going to have company in a few days."

"Company?"

"Amber. Chris has to be out of town, and he asked me to look after her. I've been running around getting her room ready. She isn't a little girl any more. I want it to be *mature* enough for her."

Tanner's gray eyes darkened. "Did you offer or did he ask?"

"He asked, but he knew I'd say yes."

"I imagine he did. He's pulling your strings, you know."

"Tanner," Melaine warned. "What I do is none of your concern."

"Maybe. Look, I've got to get back to work, but I want to talk to you about this. I've got to say my piece." He stepped back, his hands hanging loose and strong and easy by his side. "There's a new restaurant opening on Lakeview Boulevard. The owner asked me to drop by and try them out. Join me? We can talk then."

She didn't want to. Still, if she didn't, he'd know she was avoiding him. And with Amber coming in a few days, she wanted things resolved between Tanner and her. That, she told herself, was the only reason she took him up on his offer.

You're a bastard, old man, Tanner muttered to himself as he waited for Melaine to join him at the restaurant. *You have no business putting her through this.* But maybe he didn't have a choice in the matter.

The other night he'd told her that the only person he could be true to was himself. Only, he cared about Melaine.

He worried about her.

As had happened when he spotted her at the party, he knew when she walked into the restaurant. Her gold-tinted brown hair floated around her shoulders, setting off her white sweater. She wore slim slacks with the pleats that skimmed her hips. A few minutes ago he'd been aware of the restaurant's rustic decor complete with wagon wheels and cowboy sketches, but now that faded away. He thought of nothing except the wonder of having this particular woman walk back into his life.

The question was what the hell was he supposed to do about it.

"It's nice," Melaine said as she sat down. "The restaurant I mean."

"These places all try so hard, but I guess they have to do something to stand out. No last-minute emergencies? You got out of the clinic on time?"

Melaine told him about an older woman who'd come in just as she was closing. He asked what the woman's reaction had been to Melaine's recommendation that she buy shoes that fit, no matter whether they were in style or not. "She didn't say," Melaine explained. "But those blisters were making her so miserable that I think she's at least going to give it serious consideration. I gave her a pretty strong lecture about the possibility of infection. You don't really want to hear about this."

"Yes I do. I was thinking that being in the medical profession calls for a lot more than working with the human body. You have to understand where they're coming from, what's operating inside them."

"Yes." Melaine drew out the word, her eyes on him. "I do. I just thought of something. Chris never once said anything like that."

"I'm not Chris."

"I know you aren't. I'm sorry. Maybe I shouldn't have brought him up."

Tanner shrugged. "Don't be sorry. We can't help it if the man exists."

When the waitress came by, he ordered a beer for himself, noting that Melaine selected white wine. He supposed he should concentrate on the menu, but that could come later—after he'd dealt with what he believed had to be said.

Melaine was quiet. Was that because she'd anticipated him? Probably. He began by asking when she expected Amber to arrive. "Thursday," she said, her eyes shining. "For at least a week."

"Do you think it's going to happen again?"

"Again?" Melaine frowned. "What do you mean?"

"You said Chris's business is really taking off. Does that mean he's going to be doing a lot of traveling?"

"I don't know." Melaine lifted her wineglass to her lips. "I suppose so. If he does, he's going to have to work out something permanent for Amber. Either that or . . ."

When Melaine's voice faded, Tanner didn't rush filling the silence. He wondered if she had any idea how much her eyes were giving away. A moment ago, they'd glistened with excitement at the thought of seeing the girl. Now, they'd darkened. He had the uneasy feeling he knew what was on her mind. He didn't want to hear it.

But when she spoke again, he had no choice except to ride out her dream.

"I asked him, when we were going through the divorce, I begged him to give me some custody rights." Melaine set down her glass but kept her fingers wrapped around it. He noted their restless movement. "I would have done anything for that, but he—"

She was fighting back tears. He ached to be able to free her of her pain but knew that was beyond him. She loved the little girl. He understood that.

He also believed that that relationship would always color her life in dark hues.

"You asked for custody rights?" he asked gently. "But she isn't your child."

"Not biologically, but in every other way that counts."

"I understand," he said, feeling his way. "You love her. But Chris isn't willing to share custody, is he?"

"No."

"So—" Damn. He might get his head chopped off for speaking. "I guess what I don't understand is why you're putting yourself through this. I know you said that what you feel for her can't be turned off. But, Melaine, you're never going to be her mother. Chris won't let that happen. Why can't you build a separate, viable life for yourself? Cut the cord and get it over with?"

Melaine's knuckles turned white. Tanner tensed, not knowing what to expect. "Cut the cord?" she whispered, the words a painful cry. "Turn my back on Amber? You might as well kill me."

"Not me," he tried to point out. "I'm not the one who created this situation. I'm—what I'm trying to say is that I don't see how you can carve out a life of your own as long as you tie yourself to an impossible dream. As long as you draw out the heartache."

He could see her body sag. He hated himself and every word he'd spoken. But, damn it, someone had to make her understand what she was doing. It looked as if it would have to be him. After all, hadn't he been there when she'd been so shattered she couldn't speak?

"I'm sorry," he said, alive with the need to take her hand but sensing she wasn't ready to be touched. "I don't want to be cruel. That's the last thing I want. But there's something I have to ask. What would happen to your relationship with Amber if Chris remarried?"

"Marry? He—there isn't anyone in his life."

"At least not as far as you know. Come on, Melaine, surely you've considered that."

Her head came up and her spine stiffened. Still, Tanner didn't miss the raw fear lashing her. "You're saying I'm sticking my head in the sand, aren't you?" she challenged. "That I'm trying to create some kind of fairy tale life."

"Are you?"

"No! I—if Chris was to remarry, that wouldn't change anything." She stared at him with huge, trapped eyes. "Amber loves me. I'm a vital part of her world. Chris understands that."

"Does he? Look, Melaine, I don't like doing this to you any more than you like hearing it. But I think someone has to play devil's advocate here. It looks as if it's going to be me."

"Why?" She grabbed a napkin, immediately poking a hole through it with her nail. "Why these questions when—"

"When you'd like to go on with your head in the sand?"

"I told you. It's not like that at all."

"Isn't it?" Tanner pressed. Last year he'd had to fire an employee because, despite his obvious love of his job, the man wasn't dependable. Telling the twenty-one-year-old that he didn't have the necessary maturity to accept responsibility hadn't been easy. Compared to what he was doing now, that had been a cakewalk. "You just told me that nothing would change between you and Amber if she had a stepmother. I don't see how you can possibly believe that. That woman wouldn't want you in her life any more than you'd want her. Think about how confused that would make Amber. She'd be torn between two women, the one she lives with, and another she loves."

"Tanner."

Melaine's strangled whisper tore at him. Still, knowing he couldn't back off now, he took the mangled napkin out of her hand and continued. "Look at what just happened. You changed jobs, moved, so you could remain near Amber. Did Chris take you into consideration when he decided to move his business to Bishop? No. You're the one who had to accommodate him. I just don't see him putting you, or even his daughter, before his wants and desires. If he cared about that, he would have given you some kind of custody rights."

Get up. Walk out of here.

Only, Melaine couldn't do that. With Tanner's dusky eyes probing at her, she had no choice but to weather his words. "You don't understand," she whispered.

"Yes I do," he whispered back. He spread his hand over hers; she didn't know how she felt about that, but she couldn't concentrate enough to pull away. "I understand you love Amber, and putting her out of your life would tear you apart. But, Melaine, what I'm asking is, wouldn't it have been easier to have made the break a clean one at the time of the divorce? You're living in a kind of limbo. And the way I see it, you're asking Amber to do the same. She loves you. You're an important influence in her life. Maybe the most important one. And yet you have no claim to her. What kind of message is she getting?"

Melaine wanted to scream at Tanner to shut up. She didn't need to hear this!

And yet, in that secret, protected place where emotion was born and nurtured, she knew that Tanner was putting voice to something she'd never allowed herself to face.

He'd spoken the truth.

Only, he didn't understand.

Not trying to hide the tears welling in her eyes, Melaine pulled her hand free and faced Tanner. The light in the restaurant was subdued, barely aided by the candle at the corner of the table. A lover's candle. Only, Tanner had been her love just once, in another lifetime, and this was now.

And there were things she had to tell him.

"I can't shut off love . . ." she began, wishing there was some way she could speak without pain punctuating every word. "What I feel for Amber isn't going to die the way what you felt for Carla did."

Tanner clamped his lips together but didn't say anything.

"Amber and I have bonded. That'll never change."

"That's not what I said. What—"

"I know what you said," she interrupted. "I also know what's going on in my heart. It began the first day I saw Amber, and nothing you or anyone else says can alter that. It's beyond my ability to change. Do you understand that?"

"Even if it causes both of you pain?"

Melaine's head pounded. She felt as if she was about to have an accident. The skidding of tires, the relentless forward thrust of the automobile was beyond her control. Slow motion, she sensed herself hurtling into a nightmare. Here, in this restaurant, the only defense she had was words. "Tanner, I've committed myself to Amber. I know you believe I've made a mistake. Some of what you said— I know you're trying to make me look at it from your point of view because you think you're right. But you don't know me. You don't understand the kind of person I am, or what made me this way."

"No. I don't. Because we don't know each other well enough."

That hurt. Still, because of what she had to say, Melaine managed to cast his words aside. And yet it took her a few minutes to gather the courage to continue. "I understand certain things about commitment. Things that were embedded in me years ago."

"What kind of things?"

He could have tried to change the subject. The fact that he hadn't made it a little easier for her to go on. "You know what the psychology courses say. That our childhood plays a major influence on what kind of people we turn out to be. It's true for me." Why was she saying this? What was important was getting on with the telling.

"I, ah, I have two younger sisters."

"Yes."

Yes. Such a simple word, and yet it was exactly the right one. "They look up to me. They always have. I love them and feel responsible for them. I—" Damn. She had to stop stalling like this. "Tanner, something happened when I was a child, something that might explain why I'm the way I am about Amber."

When he went on leaning forward, waiting for her to continue, Melaine glanced around, wondering where the waitress had gone. But maybe they weren't going to be interrupted. Maybe she'd wind up telling him everything. "I told you that my parents were divorced when I was young, that I haven't seen my father for years. My mother—sometimes I think, if she could have found a way, she would have walked out on my sisters and myself when my father did."

"Melaine. Why?"

He went from cruel and probing to gentle so quickly. His ability to do that kept her off balance and barely able to concentrate. "I think, I guess some mothers simply aren't meant to be parents. The ability to have children doesn't mean they have that instinct."

"Your mother was one of those women without that instinct?"

At his question, Melaine nodded. Her head still pounded, but now that she'd committed herself to what had to be said, she found the going easier.

"It wasn't that she didn't try. And what I said about her wanting to walk out on us, I don't know if that's true. We gave her life a certain focus—"

"You said something happened."

"Yes." Melaine took a moment to connect with Tanner's eyes in the dim light. He seemed ageless, a mix of the wisdom of age and the curiosity of youth. Did he know that about himself? "I'd just turned ten. My mother went somewhere. I don't remember where. She left my sister and me with a neighbor. She—she didn't come back."

"What?"

"For three days. She was supposed to be gone a few hours, and she didn't come back for three days."

Melaine took a deep breath, waiting for the words to sink in. She wasn't sure whether she or Tanner needed that time. "I think, I guess she simply needed to be by herself. Or maybe there was a man. I don't know. After the first day, our neighbor decided she had to do something. She couldn't go on caring for us, not when she had children of her own to feed. She—she took us to the police."

"The police? Why?"

"I don't know." Back then those considerations hadn't mattered to her. Didn't Tanner understand that the only thing a ten-year-old girl cared about was that her mother hadn't come home? "I remember—I'll never forget sitting in the police station, on this horribly hard and uncomfortable bench, with my sisters on either side of me. I was ten years old and I was all they had to hold on to."

"Damn her."

Tanner's oath shocked her, not because it was unexpected, but because it mirrored what she'd long thought and never been able to voice. "They were crying. I tried to stop them, but I didn't know how."

"Damn her. What happened to you?"

"Foster homes." Despite the security afforded by those people who'd opened their homes to these girls, the words tasted vile on her tongue. "The police took us to a foster home."

"But your mother came back."

"Yes. But there are rules, regulations." The restaurant had filled up. It had been nearly empty when she arrived. Why hadn't she been aware of sounds and bodies? "We were assigned a social worker. That woman decided we should stay in a home until— I'm not sure. It was supposed to be only for a short while, I guess until Mother pulled herself back together. But it didn't happen. We spent years filtering in and out of foster homes."

"I guess . . ." Tanner drew out the words, carrying her along with the sound. "I guess it's a good thing they had something like that for you."

"Yes," Melaine admitted. "It was. But, Tanner, don't you see? All my sisters had was me. I—I didn't have anyone to lean on. Anyone to hold me." She'd been looking around the room, not really focusing. Now she willed herself to concentrate on Tanner. "I will not let Amber grow up like that. As long as she's alive, she'll have me."

What had they had for dinner? Tanner found that easier to think about than what Melaine had said. Only, he didn't have a clue what the waitress had put in front of him.

Now they were standing in the parking lot while Melaine dug for her car keys. He wished he'd picked her up at her place so they could leave together. At the same time, he was glad he wouldn't have to confront the incredibly complex question of whether she would ask him in. Or whether he'd accept.

"It's getting colder," he said when she shivered.

"Yes. And the nights are getting longer."

"You brought enough warm clothing? And insulated boots? I'm glad you're driving something that'll handle the snow." Christ! Couldn't he think of anything except that to say?

"I'll have to make sure Amber has what she needs. The way she's been growing—"

Although she'd given him the opening to take the conversation back to what hadn't been resolved in the restaurant, Tanner didn't say anything. She'd found her keys. He watched as she unlocked the door and pulled it open. In a moment she'd slip behind the wheel and drive out of his life.

What was he thinking? They'd see each other again, soon.

And yet—if he didn't say something, now, maybe they'd never come this close again. She'd entrusted him with so much tonight, opened up her past to him. He hadn't said much except to ask what the various foster homes had been like, what her sisters were doing, and whether the upheaval in her life had affected her schooling. Those things hadn't mattered, not really.

What he should have done was encourage her to talk more about what sitting in a police station with her sisters clinging to her had done to her.

Only, he knew.

"Don't go. Not yet."

She turned and looked up at him, making him feel both

strong and weak. "I—maybe you didn't want to hear all that," she whispered. "I haven't told many people."

"I'm glad you did," he said. It was the truth. "Everyone needs to unload."

"That's not why I did it, Tanner."

No. Of course it wasn't. What she'd told him went beyond catharsis. He started to say he understood that, but somehow the words faded off into nothing. She was still looking up at him, shivering a little, looking small and fragile and very, very desirable.

The night wind had hardened her nipples. They pushed against her sweater. She wrapped her arms around herself, and he thought about how slender her waist was. He'd climbed a mountain with her. He knew about the strength in her legs. He'd felt her calves and thighs brushing against him at the hot springs.

And three years ago he'd learned everything he needed to know about her body.

Only it wasn't enough. What he'd had three years ago wouldn't get him through tonight. Or the incredibly hard act of telling her good night.

"I'd like to think we can be friends," he said, wincing. "I'm glad you felt comfortable enough to tell me what you did."

"Friends?"

Stupid. Stupid. They'd once been lovers. That single word and everything that went with it swirled around them, coloring what they were to each other. They might be many things, but not simply friends. "People who can talk to each other," he tried again. "Who can share things."

"Do you think so?"

He didn't know. He wasn't that wise. The only thing he was sure of was that, before they parted, he had to feel her against him. Had to share something.

Run. Just run, Melaine thought. Only, when Tanner pulled her into his arms and lowered his head, asking, she didn't do that. Instead she rose onto her toes and lifted her head to ease his journey. She reached for his shoulders, gripping them, bringing herself into his warmth.

She stopped shivering the moment their lips touched. Feeling the danger, the promise, the magic, she increased the contact. He did the same, his body hard and heated. Something of him melted into her; she sensed something of her blending into him. Forcing down a sigh that would have sounded like surrender, she simply clung. Kissed him.

Accepted and gave. Silent. That way neither of them would be tempted to try to explain what was happening.

That way she wouldn't be forced to face a word she didn't understand or believe in.

EIGHT

Although it had begun to snow when Bert took off for Bishop, he assured Melaine he'd be back before a few flakes turned into something to worry about. Melaine knew he was right; still, she was relieved when, a little more than an hour later, he taxied into the airport. Amber, who fairly dove from the plane into Melaine's arms, was beside herself with excitement. Not only did she declare flying the most thrilling thing she'd ever done, but she was determined to get her pilot's license as soon as she was old enough.

They drove to Melaine's place in a rapidly building snowstorm which delighted Amber almost as much as flying had. It wasn't until she'd been in the A-frame the better part of an hour that she noticed the spare room Melaine had transformed into a girl's world. "Awesome," Amber proclaimed. She stood with her hands planted on her hips, looking up at the picture over her bed. "I'm going to stay here forever."

Melaine didn't bother to correct her.

The next morning Melaine took Amber to work with her. She thought Amber might become bored, but Amber busied herself by acting as receptionist, informing her steady stream of patients that they were under the best of care and if they were scared, she'd hold their hand. Several people took her up on her offer. When Melaine asked, Amber explained that she'd told Andy where she'd be, and Andy had wanted to come with her. "I don't know," Amber said hugging Melaine. "I miss Andy, but I want it to be just you and me."

"So do I, honey. So do I."

Just the same, in the afternoon Melaine called Carol to ask if she and Bert wanted to come over for dinner. They could all look at the mule deer pictures.

"I'd love to meet your young friend, but Bert already invited Tanner to drop over for a beer after work. Maybe—"

Before giving herself time for second thoughts, Melaine included Tanner in her invitation. She hadn't seen or talked to him since their kiss in the parking lot. Having the Edmondses and Amber around should ease her passed any awkwardness with Tanner. Somehow she had to find the right opportunity to tell him she didn't want that to happen again.

Kissing Tanner made her feel too many things she didn't understand.

Tanner hadn't given much thought to what the little girl would be like. He supposed he should have, but knowing he'd see Melaine got in the way of other matters. When Bert knocked on Melaine's door and then guided his wife inside, Tanner held back.

The house smelled like sauteeing onions, heating briquettes, lavender.

Lavender?

When a long-legged, long-armed girl with shoulder-length blond hair and a half shy, half-inquisitive grin slowly extended her hand to him, he realized the lavender scent came from her. He knew better than to point out that a lighter touch with perfume would have done the trick. He also wasn't going to mention that jeans and perfume made for an interesting "blend."

"I know who you are," Amber said, peeking up at him from under lashes that one day would knock the boys off their feet. "Melaine said you make sure people don't get hurt when they're skiing. Do you really set off dynamite?"

"When I need to, but that's only part of what I do."

"I know." Amber nodded wisely. "You find people if they get lost and tell them if there's going to be a blizzard and—do you have a rescue dog?"

Intrigued by the girl's enthusiasm, Tanner sat down on the couch and did his best to answer her questions. When Melaine came in with a beer and handed it to him, he looked at her over Amber's head but didn't make the mistake of dismissing the animated girl. He might not have much experience with children, but he understood that his attention was important to her. Amber was trying to size him up. He owed it to her to treat her questions seriously. He and Melaine could talk later—if they could find anything to talk about.

That happened after dinner when Melaine brought out the pictures she'd taken from Bert's plane and she and Bert launched into an explanation of what they'd experienced.

"I couldn't believe it," Melaine enthused. "I've never seen that many deer all in one place." She handed Tanner a photograph of two large bucks emerging from the brush. "These two—they look invincible."

Tanner agreed. He wished he'd been there to share in her delight. "I can't see a fawn without remembering going to see *Bambi*. I must have been seven or eight. My mom took me and some kids from the neighborhood. I could hear her sniffling when Bambi's mother died. I swore I wouldn't cry, but I blew it. Had to get up and walk out into the lobby."

Melaine's smile was all the reward he needed for revealing a childhood secret. It bothered him to know she'd probably never had that kind of memory of her mother.

To distract her, and maybe himself, he told her about his one and only hunting trip. When it came to sight down his rifle at a buck, he knew he'd never be able to pull the trigger. "Embarrassed the heck out of my dad. We'd gone with his brother. All that macho male talk, and I refused to shoot. Fortunately, my dad's a forgiving man. My uncle still brings that up, but then I point out that he couldn't hit the broad side of a barn."

Smiling, Melaine inclined closer to him on the couch. "It was the Bambi movie," she said softly. "It ruined you for hunting. I'm glad." From out of the corner of his eye, Tanner noticed Amber's reaction.

The little girl understood. Oh, maybe she didn't fully comprehend how complicated his and Melaine's relationship was, but from the way her body tensed, he knew she sensed that something more than friendship was involved. Maybe he should have taken that as his cue and treated Melaine as nothing more than a cook and hostess, but he didn't. He couldn't. Amber would have to understand that.

Carol chose a couple of pictures she wanted enlarged and then asked Amber which ones she preferred. "You could have them hung in the room Melaine has for you, or you could take them home with you."

"Here," Amber declared. "I like the baby deer the best."

"So do I," Carol agreed, and then told Amber she was going to have a baby. For a minute Amber simply stared at Carol's stomach.

"Can you feel it?" she asked.

"Not yet," Carol admitted. Alerted by something that might have been nothing more than the instinct he felt around her, Tanner glanced over at Melaine. She was smiling, but the gesture didn't reach her eyes.

She wants a child.

Shaken by the thought, Tanner fought to concentrate on the questions Amber was asking about babies. Whether

Melaine wanted a baby or not was none of his business, nothing that involved him. And yet, in a primitive, unthinking way he wanted to be able to give her that.

Amber, no matter how much Melaine loved the girl, wasn't her child.

And yet there was no denying the strength of that relationship. As the evening wore on and the conversation touched on everything from learning to skiing to what Amber expected from school, Tanner came to understand how deeply the current of love from Melaine to Amber flowed. They were comfortable in each other's presence. There was no sense that Melaine had to struggle to reach Amber on her level. And Amber obviously cared about Melaine's life. Twice Melaine reminded Amber to lower her voice. Amber wrinkled up her nose at that but complied—just as any cooperative child would around her mother.

A little after 9 P.M., Carol and Amber both began to droop. When Bert suggested it was time they leave, Tanner helped Carol to her feet and then shook Amber's hand solemnly. "If you're serious about learning how to ski, I can fix you up with someone who works with a lot of kids," he offered.

"Melaine's going to teach me. She promised."

Something about Amber's response held Tanner's attention. He glanced first at Melaine, who didn't seem to have heard. When he looked down at Amber, he saw that the wary look had returned.

Amber wasn't at ease with him. She didn't trust him.

Why? It wasn't as if he was going to rob her of Melaine's time and attention, or affection.

No. Nothing like that.

But Amber had been open and friendly at the beginning. It was only later, when he and Melaine were sitting near each other on the couch, that Amber had pulled back.

* * *

It snowed almost continually for the next four days. During that time snowplows worked to keep the roads clear, Melaine unpacked a few late-supply deliveries and taught Amber how to ski—according to Amber, well enough that she was ready to start preparing for the next Olympics. She wanted to tell her father since he'd never found time to put her on a pair of skis. On the fifth day, the word went out. Mammoth Lakes, California, was officially open for business.

That afternoon Melaine had her first ski-related accident, a middle-aged woman with a badly wrenched knee. Tanner brought her into the clinic and stayed with her until her husband could be found.

"So much for their weekend," Tanner said after helping the man deposit his wife in their car. "She's going to be out of commission for a while, is she?"

"I'm afraid so," Melaine said as, with Amber's help, she straightened the examination room. "She's going to have to stay off that knee for a while. Still, I think she was more embarrassed than anything. She told me she'd been bragging for weeks that she's better on skis than her husband."

"From the way he was talking, I don't think he'll hold that over her." Tanner folded the wheelchair he'd used to get the woman up the ramp and into the clinic. "You've had a few days of pretty cold weather. Do you think the heat here is going to be adequate?"

Melaine assured him that she hadn't detected any drafts and that the gas heat kept the clinic at an even, comfortable temperature. When he first arrived, Tanner had been preoccupied with his charge's needs, but now he seemed relaxed. And in no hurry to leave.

She wasn't sure how she felt about that. The other night, with the Edmondses and Amber around, had taught her that she could never be near Tanner without being aware of him. He'd shed his parka and run broad fingers through his damp hair. Still, those gestures hadn't lessened the sense that she was sharing the clinic with a mountain man. Maybe if she stayed on the far side of the examination table—

"Was she heavy?"

Melaine looked over at Amber. How could she have forgotten that the girl was here?

"Not very," Tanner explained. "I know how to carry her so I won't hurt my back."

"Oh." Amber looked up at Tanner as if taking her measure of him. "If you lifted Melaine, would she be heavy?"

"No. Not at all."

"But you don't have to because she doesn't have a hurt knee."

"Would it bother you if I did?" Tanner asked.

Melaine frowned. What point was he trying to make? She watched Amber shuffle from one foot to the other, resenting the fact that Tanner had made Amber uncomfortable. Still, she said nothing because she sensed that this conversation was between Tanner and Amber, that there were things the two needed to discover about each other.

"You don't have to," Amber said. "She's a grown-up."

"Yes. She is. But sometimes grown-ups like to get close to each other even if neither of them is hurt. You understand that, don't you?"

"Y-es," Amber admitted reluctantly. "But you don't know Melaine very well."

"What makes you say that?"

"Because she hasn't been here very long. And she came all by herself."

A faint smile touched Tanner's lips. He lifted his hand as if to touch Amber, then let it drop. "That was pretty brave of her, wasn't it? Going somewhere where she didn't have any friends. You did the same thing when you moved to Bishop. But you've made friends, haven't you? Melaine's doing the same."

Amber looked as if she wasn't quite sure of that. "I had my daddy with me. But he's awfully busy. At first I didn't like the other kids, but that was before I got to know them."

"Exactly. Melaine and I, we're getting to know each other."

Amber stared, first at Tanner and then at Melaine. Uncharacteristically, she shuffled from one leg to the other. "Are you going to get married?"

"Married?" Melaine stammered as Tanner gave her a "where did this come from" look. "What makes you ask that?"

" 'Cause . . ." Amber stared at the floor. " 'Cause Daddy said you might get married someday."

Melaine felt as if her heart had been punctured. She could only clasp Amber to her. "He—did? Did he—did he say what would happen then?"

Amber nodded, her body jerking. "Then you'd—you'd have your own family, and you wouldn't have time for me anymore."

When Melaine shot Tanner an anguished look, his eyes were filled with compassion. She'd been fighting to accept the fact that Tanner objected to her relationship with Amber. But now she saw another side to him.

No matter what he believed, he could still feel for a motherless child.

"That's never going to happen," Melaine whispered, still holding Amber. "Never. Honey, that's the most important promise I'll ever make you."

"Really?"

"Really," she repeated. She didn't look at Tanner again.

How or why she wound up inviting Tanner to join them for dinner, Melaine wasn't quite sure. All she knew was that it was important that the three of them spend time together. Amber needed to understand that Tanner's presence didn't mean she would be shunted aside. Tanner and Amber needed to get to know each other.

And even if she didn't understand her emotions, she needed Tanner.

"Anything except a casserole," he said when she asked what he wanted for dinner. "In the early days of my bachelorhood, I experimented with a lot of them, thinking that was an easy way to lump all the food groups together. Bad idea."

Melaine laughed and helped Amber onto the counter so the girl could supervise dinner preparations. "There are casseroles and then there are casseroles. If I were you, I'd avoid anything that calls for cream of mushroom soup. Everything tends to taste the same that way. Amber, you decide."

Amber, who'd just gotten off the phone with Andy, seemed to have regained her upbeat approach toward life. She regarded Tanner for several seconds and then voted for Mexican food. "I like cheese the best," she explained.

Tanner nodded. "So do I."

A half hour later the three of them had come up with a variation of taco salad. Tanner pretended to take elaborate notes on how the dish was prepared. When he started to write down pickles and cauliflower, Amber, laughing, corrected him. They ate picnic-style in the living room while watching a comedy Amber enjoyed.

Still, Melaine noted that Amber sat between her and Tanner on the couch, so close to her that she could barely use her arm. Amber was a bright girl. She must have picked up on the current flowing between the adults.

The current was strong. Even as the three of them laughed over the argument between the show's characters, a part of Melaine remained removed from the TV, tuned into Tanner's presence. While they were at the clinic, her protective sense where Amber was concerned had kicked into gear. Tanner had tried to push Amber to explore her feelings; Melaine hadn't wanted that. But during the process of cooking and eating dinner, the unease between these two important people in her life had faded, leaving her free to concentrate on what she felt whenever Tanner was around.

She remembered that magical, lost night. Even now, her body felt wired. He'd been an incredible lover: gentle, sure. How he'd sensed that she'd needed time before committing to the act of ultimate intimacy she didn't know. What had made the night enchanted was that he'd been so wise. When she hadn't understood her body and heart's needs, he'd found ways to tap into her, take her out of herself.

In his arms she'd found release from agony. Found the path to ecstasy.

She wanted—dear God—she needed that again.

Just that. Only that.

In an effort to fend off her restlessness, Melaine suggested that since it was snowing lightly, they could bundle up and build a snowman in the dark. Tanner looked at her as if she'd taken leave of her senses, but Amber thought her idea *absolutely* wonderful. Grumbling a little, Tanner finally agreed.

The three of them spent an hour creating a six-foot-high snowman at the side of the A-frame. Tanner did most of the physical labor while Melaine and Amber worked on creating a figure with personality. By the time they finished, the snowman had been draped in a long, brightly colored scarf, gardening hat, and a "belt" made of several old towels twisted together. Facial features had been created from chocolate chips.

"Perfect," Melaine proclaimed at last. Her feet, despite her boots, were numb. Her nose felt as if it would break off, and she could barely move her fingers inside the now-wet gloves. At least Amber didn't look or act cold, thanks in part to the insulated red gloves Melaine had bought yesterday. In fact, Amber announced that the snowman looked lonely and needed company.

"Why don't you wait until tomorrow," Tanner suggested. "I might have a baseball cap around you can use. Besides . . ." He began steering Amber toward the house. "I'm an old man. I'm only good for one snowman a night."

Once inside, Melaine concentrated on getting Amber out of her clothes and into a soft flannel nightgown. By then Tanner had shed his jacket and was in the kitchen preparing hot chocolate. Shivering, Melaine stripped off her wet things. She turned up the heat before joining Tanner.

He looked at peace in her kitchen. The thought unnerved her, leaving her wondering at her reaction. Chris had had a domestic side in that he liked experimenting with exotic dishes—leaving her to do the cleaning up. Now Tanner was doing nothing more complex than stirring envelopes of chocolate mix into hot water; yet, he looked far more comfortable with himself than Chris ever had.

"Wonderful," Melaine said as warm liquid eased away her chill. "My compliments to the chef."

Tanner had been on his way into the living room with marshmallow-topped hot chocolate for Amber. He stopped at the doorway and turned back. His eyes remained on her face, but she sensed the effort it took. The electricity she'd felt earlier had been cooled by the snow; it returned now. She wasn't the only one who felt it.

He spoke slowly. "Thank you for asking me over. I wasn't sure."

"What weren't you sure about?" she asked when he didn't go on.

"Whether you wanted me. You sensed the tension between Amber and me, didn't you?"

Because Amber was once again settled in front of the TV, Melaine felt sure the girl wouldn't hear. "She was uncomfortable thinking about us together. You could have sidestepped that. Why didn't you?"

"I might ask why you had me over tonight. If you don't want her seeing us together—"

"I can't shelter her from the world," Melaine interrupted. As soon as she said the words, she understood. Tanner had pressed Amber to talk about her feelings because avoiding the issue wouldn't make it go away. He'd just done the same to her. "I'm sorry," she said softly. "I can't help being protective around her. You don't know her the way I do. You don't know what she can handle, and what she can't."

"In other words, it's all right for the three of us to build a snowman together, but I can't talk to her about anything more serious than a chocolate-chip mouth unless you give permission?"

Melaine's head ached. Whether from the complexity of the conversation or as a result of the war going on inside her simply because she was close to him, she didn't know. "Tanner, when Amber's with me, she's my responsibility. My concern. She's nothing to you."

"Isn't she? Melaine, whether I think it's right or not, she's part of your world. And the fact is, you and I are part of each other's world."

Melaine wasn't interested in continuing the conversation. Not with Amber in the next room and the simple fact of Tanner's presence adding its own layers. "Amber's going to wonder where we are," she said, and slid past him into the living room. She still felt cold, all except her left arm. That had touched Tanner's chest.

Amber was staring wide-eyed at the TV, but her sagging lower lip told Melaine that it wouldn't be long before the girl fell asleep. Melaine sat next to her and wrapped her arm around her, giving Amber something to lean against. Tanner settled himself in a chair, obviously in no hurry to leave.

A half hour later, Amber was asleep. Although she should have taken her to bed, Melaine held her a little longer, letting the wonderful feel of that warm, soft little body soak into her. She ran her lips over the top of Amber's head and breathed in what remained of lavender perfume.

Tanner got to his feet. Melaine looked up at him, unsure of what he had in mind. He reached for Amber. "Let me," he whispered.

Although she worried that being in a strange man's arms might wake Amber, Melaine let him carry her up the stairs and into her bedroom. "There's something about a sleeping child," Tanner whispered as Melaine pulled back the covers. "The sense of trust in a small, limp body."

Melaine waited until they'd backed out of the room. "Don't you understand?" she whispered. "That's why I can't imagine life without her."

"Melaine." Tanner touched her, stopping her from stepping away from him. "I want you to be happy. You deserve it. I want the same for her. But I look at the two of you together and think about what's going to happen when you're torn apart. What I'm saying is, get it over. Now. Before it gets any harder."

No! She'd heard those words from Tanner before. She wasn't going to listen to them again. Melaine pulled free and took the stairs as rapidly as she could. She looked around, trying to find Tanner's coat. She finally remembered that he'd left it hung over the back of a kitchen chair.

Although it was still damp, she handed it to him. "This isn't getting us anywhere," she managed through nerveless lips. "You don't understand. You don't even try to understand!"

"The hell I don't." Tanner took his coat, then flung it back over the chair. He gripped Melaine's elbows and pulled her closer. "Look, when I heard that you'd come here, I wanted to drive out of Mammoth and never come back. Only, I didn't. I told myself that we're adults, that we could work out a sane and sensible relationship. I'm still willing to try."

Melaine didn't bother struggling. She knew her strength

wasn't enough to counter his. "What are you saying? That this disagreement—whatever it is—is all my fault?"

"You tell me."

"Don't," she warned.

"All right." He sighed but didn't release her. "What we did—the night we spent together—it wasn't real."

"I know that."

"Something took over there. Chemistry. Make believe. Something that had nothing to do with the real world and had never happened to either of us before."

"Yes." He still held her, his hands now inching up her arms.

"I didn't question. I just let it happen."

"So—did I."

"It was insane, Melaine. Insane. We didn't know each other."

"No."

"And it isn't going to happen again."

"No." Having to say that brought her close to tears. Yet, he was right. "It won't." She forced out the words. "Now you know who I am. The complications in my life."

"Just as you know that I failed in my one attempt at marriage and take my work very seriously and have strong opinions about your relationship with Amber."

She felt his breath on her cheek and the side of her nose. She felt his heat seeping into her breasts. Her stomach knotted with something she recognized but didn't want to put a name to. "We can't go back. And there's nothing for us now."

"No. Nothing."

Only, his body wasn't saying that. He'd pulled her closer, imprinting her with his presence. Or had she been the one to make the move? He smelled of damp denim and chocolate. She remembered how he looked bent over a massive snowball, his black hair touched by the light from her porch. She tried to free herself from that captivating image only to find herself face-to-face with the memory of the look in his eyes as he tucked Amber's blankets around her neck.

She could love a man like that.

No. What was she thinking? Love for a man was something she'd never held in her hands. Never come close to experiencing. With Tanner leaning over her, his fingers pressed into her back, she tried to tell herself there was nothing between them, nothing for them.

She couldn't form the words.

"You're a witch, Melaine," he whispered, warm, moist breath penetrating the hair around her temple to kiss her flesh. "Every time I look at you, it happens."

"What . . ." She shouldn't be running her hands up his arms, finding the strong, solid set of his shoulders. She shouldn't lean into him. Still . . . "What happens?"

"Insanity." Inch by inch, his mouth closed in on her. "I can't call it anything else."

She wasn't a witch. He was the one with all the power. Only, telling him that meant being able to speak, and she'd forgotten how. The knot in her stomach twisted and heated, spreading lower, lower. She felt her legs wash weak and strong by turn. A bold woman, a powerful woman would wrench herself out of this warlock's arms.

Melaine was neither of those things. If there was any power in the room, it belonged to him.

When, after what seemed a lifetime of wanting, she pressed her body against his and lifted her face for the kiss she needed as much as she needed life itself, Melaine knew the battle had been lost.

That she hadn't even tried to fight.

He'd spread his hands over her back. Now he pressed the tips of his fingers inward, finding that incredibly sensitive spot at the base of her spine. A shock of electricity centered in her there before spiraling outward.

Mindless, Melaine parted her lips. Her tongue inched, tentative, from between her teeth. When, still uncertain, she touched his mouth, she found her reward. He allowed her access. Growing bolder, she explored that warm, damp place. She tried to concentrate. Somehow it was terribly, terribly important that she understand what he was capable of doing to her.

But there was so much. His fingers on her spine, his male body pressed against hers, the rise and fall of his chest which became her own movement . . . She lost herself.

Hands on her hips. When had that happened?

Hands sliding lower, reaching the uppermost curve of her thighs, strong fingers spreading outward, pulling her ever closer.

And somehow, through it all, the deepening, powerful kiss.

Melaine groaned, the sound pulled from her very core. She arched into him, her own hands frantic. She clutched his neck, holding him against her, needing to give back a little of the energy he'd given her.

She needed more. Her hungry hands roamed over his neck, shoulders, down his arms, pressing tightly against the ribs just above his waist. She felt his hands still on her hips and thighs. The wonder of feeling utterly shameless overcame her.

Amber was asleep. Her bedroom, the night, was theirs. The night.

Only, after the night came morning.

It wasn't until Tanner leaned away so he could cover her breasts, imprinting her with the stroke of his fingers, that she knew how close to the edge they'd danced.

A minute longer, a few more seconds, and they'd careen over the edge.

"Tanner. Tanner."

"No."

"I have to say it. You did. We aren't anything to each other."

"Liar."

Yes, she was a liar. And her body had become a traitor to everything she'd tried to tell herself since the day she'd once again spoken the name Tanner Harris.

NINE

Amber wound up staying an extra two days because Chris's business kept him away longer than he expected. Melaine was delighted but concerned over the amount of school Amber was missing. She called Amber's school and talked to her teacher. Because Amber had brought a couple of her books with her, Melaine turned the evenings into tutoring sessions. At Carol's suggestion, she let Amber spend a day at the stables where Amber became an expert on the care and feeding of draft horses, particularly the young one called Rabbit who Amber claimed as her own.

Because skiers flocked to the slopes, Melaine saw little of Tanner. She told herself that was exactly as it should be. Something happened when they were together, something uncontrollable. Eventually, she tried to convince herself, this unreasoning physical attraction would play itself out. In the meantime, work should keep her busy.

It did. Only, not busy enough. In the evenings after putting Amber to bed, Melaine stepped outside and looked across the lake. Despite the distance and poor lighting, she knew which was Tanner's cabin. She became accustomed to his habit of walking down to the lake and standing by its edge for several minutes before turning off his outside lights. His silhouette as he neared the water faded into nothing. Still, she remained where she was until he reappeared.

She wondered if he looked for her.

She guessed that, like she, he found reasons for not calling.

Although Melaine had made tentative plans to have Bert fly Amber back to Bishop, Chris called to let her know he needed to visit a couple of the ski shops in Mammoth. "Tell Amber to get ready," he announced. "She and I are going to do a little cross-country skiing."

Amber, of course, was delighted. She wanted to show off her newfound skill. Melaine said little, but she knew Chris. He approached recreation with the same single-mindedness he did business. He'd expect Amber to keep up, even if she was only eight years old and still had a lot to learn about skiing.

She was right. "Anyone can do it," Chris announced when she expressed doubts about the cross-country area off Old Mammoth Road. "From what I've determined, all the trails are groomed. They go through a meadow, for crying out loud. There aren't any hills."

"That's not the point." Melaine kept her voice carefully neutral. "What's easy for adult legs isn't for someone Amber's age."

"You worry too much," Chris informed her, his expression warning her that, as always when it came to his daughter, he considered himself the final authority. "Someday she's going to be the spokesperson for my skis. It's time she started earning her wings."

That wasn't the point. Because Amber received so little of her father's time, she would be determined to match his pace, to earn his approval. She wouldn't be tuned into her own limits. Once again Melaine tried to talk Chris into taking a shorter trip, but he'd made up his mind.

"It isn't negotiable, Melaine," he informed her. "She's growing up. She's a trooper."

"She's still a little girl."

"She sure as hell won't be anything else if you have your way. Look, we've been over this before, and you know my stand. She's my daughter. I'm the one who makes the decisions where she's concerned."

Hiding her helpless rage, Melaine went about gathering up what Amber would need for the next several hours. Amber had been outside while the argument took place, which meant she was spared the uncomfortable scene. Not that that would have made a difference with Chris, Melaine thought. His firm belief that he knew what was best held him in good stead with his business. Unfortunately, he'd never fully understood his daughter's limits.

Melaine gave Amber a hug and smile as she left. Then, feeling the weight of what she'd just experienced, she walked over to the clinic picture window and stared up at the chair lifts now crowded with people. Her vision blurred, and she wiped away tears.

If only a patient would walk in. If only Tanner would show up. He'd agree that Amber wasn't strong enough for the lengthy, fast-paced outing Chris had in mind.

But that wouldn't be all Tanner would say. *She isn't yours. You can't run her life.*

"I know," Melaine moaned. "Oh, God, I know."

Despite a rash of minor emergencies, the afternoon dragged. Finally Melaine closed up, and although she needed to go to the grocery store, she drove directly home. Fighting tears, she went about the painful task of packing Amber's belongings so Chris and Amber could return to Bishop. Twice she paused in front of the telephone. She could call Bert and Carol or one of the other residents she'd met. She could call Tanner and tell him she didn't want to be alone.

But she didn't have the energy for her friends. And Tanner would see right through her.

When she heard a vehicle approaching, Melaine hurried outside. Chris jumped out of his side of the car and walked around to the passenger's side. He opened the door and reached in for Amber. He deposited her on her feet and stalked toward the A-frame. Amber trudged after him, her face tear-streaked. Ignoring Chris, Melaine hugged Amber to her. "What's wrong?" she asked. "Did you hurt yourself?"

"No. Daddy's mad. I made him wait and wait."

Bristling, Melaine turned on Chris. Darn it, she'd warned him! "I thought this was supposed to be relaxation," she blurted. "What's the big hurry?"

"The hurry? The point is, this was supposed to be a test of a cross-country ski prototype I designed. How am I going to know how well the skis hold up if I'm going at a snail's pace?"

Knowing Amber's determination to meet any challenge, Melaine doubted that she'd done less than her best. If Chris couldn't see that . . . "Then you should have gone with an adult, not a child," she said.

"Maybe I should have. Only . . ." Chris looked down at his daughter. "We needed some time together."

"I understand. Only, not like that."

"Don't."

Alerted by the warning tone in Chris's voice, Melaine told Amber to go inside to change. When Chris started to follow suit, she stopped him. "What do you mean, don't?" she asked.

"Don't start, Melaine. I thought we'd worked this out. You'd remain Amber's friend. I know she needs a female influence in her life. But you aren't her parent. *I* am."

Stung, Melaine could only whisper, "It could have been different."

"Yeah. I know. By me giving you custody. Only, it isn't going to happen. You know that."

Yes. She did. Weeks of pleading and begging had done her no good. Chris had no intention of giving up custody. And if Chris felt he was being pressed into a corner, the vital time she spent with Amber would be taken away. And where would Amber be? She *needed* a mother. "Give me a few minutes with her, please?" Melaine asked despite the lump in her throat which threatened to shut off speech. "I'll help her change and try to calm her down."

"I guess," Chris grumbled. "Why it turned out to be a test of wills—"

That wasn't it at all, but given Chris's present mood and her own tension, Melaine knew better than to try to point that out. Instead she focused on Amber's needs, rubbing the soreness out of her ankles and promising she'd call tomorrow.

When Chris announced that he had to leave, Melaine didn't stall the moment. Taking Amber's hand, she walked outside with her and made sure Amber put on her seat belt. She kissed her forehead, the tip of her nose, her chin, returned her strong hug, then backed away and waved until she could no longer see Amber's face in the rear window.

Feeling as if she'd been emptied out inside, Melaine walked up the steps and closed the door. She started across the living room, her mind a tangle of emotions. Then, without knowing how it happened, she collapsed on the couch and began crying.

When, a half hour later, she thought she could trust herself to speak, she picked up the phone and dialed. "Are . . . I thought—I'd like to try to prove that there is such a thing as a good casserole."

Fool.

Tanner glared at his reflection in the mirror. He ran a hot wash cloth over his face, applied shaving cream, and started shaving.

Fool.

He'd stayed away the better part of a week, hadn't he?

His argument that seeing Melaine again any time soon would be the biggest mistake of the year made an incredible amount of sense. Tromping over the mountain every day until his leg muscles cramped and his ears felt as if they would crack off had left him so tired that he'd been able to sleep. Of course there were the dreams—dreams he refused to look at under the morning light. Dreams that left him wired with wanting her.

Tanner finished with his left side and began on the right. Hadn't he spent hours, days, carefully rehearsing what he'd say when and if circumstances brought them together? *I've given it a lot of thought, Melaine. There's physical attraction between us. I don't think either of us will deny that. But we can't let that get in the way of a simple fact. We disagree about too much.* Oh, yes, it was a perfectly valid argument.

One that had gone out the window the moment he heard her anguished voice over the phone. She hadn't said anything, but he sensed that her invitation didn't have a damn thing to do with a casserole and everything to do with an empty bedroom.

She has to work it out on her own. She knows how you feel about this. If she doesn't agree—

Maybe they wouldn't talk about Amber at all. Maybe she'd tell him about her patients, how Carol's pregnancy was progressing, whether her roof leaked. He'd come up with a few anecdotes about desk jockeys determined to prove themselves against an unforgiving mountain. He'd tell her about the deer tracks he'd come across a little after dawn this morning, the lack of activity from his resident chipmunks. He'd try what she prepared and pronounce it good. They'd watch a little TV together, and then he'd come back home.

Without tasting her. Without testing his self-control.

Sure he would.

*   *   *

"It'd be better if I'd been able to use fresh vegetables," Melaine explained. "But it's hard getting them here."

"Don't worry about it. I think this is wonderful."

"Spoken like a true bachelor," Melaine said, and then wished she could take the words back. She'd worked so hard at keeping the conversation on a safe and sane level. Instead of sitting casually in the living room, she'd set the kitchen table. That way they'd have substance between them, and she wouldn't be tempted to touch him and draw from his strength. But, without meaning to, she'd brought up the simple and inescapable fact that they were both single. Alone. Together. "You said . . . you were saying we're getting more snow than normal for this early in the season. Is the removal equipment adequate to handle it?"

"That shouldn't be a problem." Tanner took a bite and gave her yet another approving smile. "Delicious. Absolutely delicious."

Although this was the third time Tanner had said that, Melaine responded as if he'd just given her the compliment. The truth was, she was thoroughly sick of talking about dinner. And the weather. Only, she didn't trust herself to approach any other conversation.

Tanner gave her a thorough rundown on the resort's snow removal equipment. She nodded and asked just enough questions that, hopefully, he believed she cared. Then, before she could prepare herself, he leaned back and met her eyes.

"She's gone, isn't she?"

"Amber? Yes."

"This afternoon?"

"Yes. Not long ago."

"Not long before you called me?"

Melaine winced. Chris had shot from the hip. Now Tanner was doing the same thing. "I wanted to thank you for the way you treated her," she said. "She's decided that no one can make a snowman quite the way you do."

"It hurts to see her leave, doesn't it? The house feels empty."

What was his point? If he was trying to make her admit that her life revolved around a child she had no claim to, his timing was horrible. "Yes," she conceded, determined not to let the pain she felt show. "But that's not the reason I invited you over. Amber and I have parted before. I'll call her tomorrow. I want to know how school went."

"Then why did you invite me over?"

He wasn't supposed to ask that, not when she didn't have an answer, at least not one she wanted to admit. "I thought . . . I wanted to know how things are going on the slopes. I feel so shut off from that in the clinic."

"Do you?" Tanner took a final bite and pushed his plate away. When Melaine reached for it, he stretched out his hand to stop her. "Let's put them in the sink. They can wait."

Of course they could. Still, if she didn't wash dishes, what would she do?

Tanner supplied that answer. Before she could get to her feet, he began collecting dishes. He took an armload to the counter and put what was left of the casserole in the refrigerator. Then, without asking permission, he placed his arm around her shoulder and guided her into the living room. She hoped, she wanted him to turn on the TV, but he didn't. Instead he drew back the drapes over the window that faced the lake and turned on the outside light. Beyond them, the lake stretched dark and quiet. Tanner sat on the couch and turned so he could look out the window. After a moment of indecision, she sat a few inches away. She felt her muscles tense.

She'd waited so long to have him with her again.

"I've heard some good things about you."

Because she was unprepared to have the conversation take that turn, it was a moment before Melaine could ask Tanner to explain himself.

"The members of my team. Several of them have

brought injured skiers to you this week. They say you're calm, that no matter how upset a patient is, you're able to get them to relax."

"It's all that experience of working in a city emergency room," Melaine explained. "Next to some of the things I've seen as a result of a gang fight, a broken leg is nothing."

"No. I guess it isn't." Tanner ran his hand over his thigh, distracting her. "I know you came here to be closer to Amber, but did the other factor in? I mean, you told me how you feel about flying over a deer herd and watching the stars reflected in Lake Mary. That isn't easy to reconcile with what you've learned of man's savage side."

Melaine took a deep breath, stalling for time. She'd tried to convince herself that he didn't know her. But, even though he'd never watched her working over a drug-crazed man bleeding from a knife wound, he knew what that experience had done to her.

"No. It wasn't easy." She picked at a piece of lint, needing something to do. "I found myself becoming calloused. Laughing at insane situations because the alternative was crying. Going into the nurses' lounge and making horrible jokes about the results of an automobile accident. I know it's an occupational hazard. The police I dealt with, the doctors, they put up the same self-protective shell that I did. But I didn't like it. I wanted to stay in touch with what I believed about myself—that I'd gotten into nursing because I care about people. And I hated the thought that what was happening to me might rub off on Amber."

At the sound of Amber's name, Tanner's eyes darkened, but he didn't say anything. Instead he got up and turned on the stereo. A woman began singing about how her life had gone from night to day because she'd met the right man. "Do you remember?" Tanner asked when he sat back down. "The night we hit all those casinos?"

Melaine went back in time. They'd held hands and

walked and watched and listened. Much of that time they'd listened to a woman with a voice like liquid thunder.

That incredible singer had held the morning world at bay, had been part of the journey from painful reality to dreams and magic. The magic hadn't lasted, but Melaine remembered. Tanner, she now knew, had done the same.

"I don't remember her name. But her voice—I've never heard anything like it. When she sang, I felt her voice flow into me, running hot and cold through me—"

"Do you really think it was the singer?"

He wasn't going to dodge the past. Maybe because it was night and beyond her window she could see snow drifting down over Lake Mary, Melaine felt strong enough to do the same. "I don't know. Maybe it was us."

"That's what I don't understand. What happened?"

We made love. Only, they'd done more than that. For a few hours she'd given Tanner Harris everything she had to give and believed he'd done the same for her. "I can't speak for you," she whispered. "I turned my back on what had brought me to Nevada. I needed to feel as if life was worth living. You—gave me that."

"Only, when the fantasy I helped create gave way before the real world, I blamed you."

This was the first time she'd heard Tanner assume responsibility for what had happened. Unsure how to accept his honesty, Melaine closed her eyes, trying to concentrate on the simple notes coming from the stereo. Yet, while her body absorbed sound, her mind held onto what he'd said. "The real world. Tanner, you asked if I left big-city nursing because I'd seen too much of the seamy side of life. Maybe that's what happened when we made love." She opened her eyes. As difficult as this was to say, she needed to face him. "We each had a dream—maybe everyone has a fantasy inside them. We want to be Cinderella and Prince Charming. We want to live in this happy-ever-after world. Neither of us knew what to do when the fantasy ended and life, real life, returned."

"It took me too damn long to realize that."

Tanner leaned forward. His body called to her. For the first time since seeing him again, she could look him in the eye and not feel the need to ask for forgiveness. They still didn't agree about the most important person in her life, but right now that didn't matter. Nothing did except the call.

"We complicate things so much, don't we?" she asked. "People make things so difficult."

"It doesn't have to be that way."

"Doesn't it?"

"No," Tanner said, and got to his feet. He stepped toward her, his presence both promise and test. "Not if we're willing to wade through all the garbage and get to the truth."

"The truth?"

Despite the A-frame's high ceiling, he seemed to be expanding, taking over every inch of space. "You told me what it was like working in Emergency and what that did to you. Now it's my turn for some honesty."

Melaine waited. Felt his sensual challenge and waited.

"I want it again. What we experienced. I want it tonight."

Melaine swallowed. For the life of her she couldn't speak, or turn away.

"I want to make love to you."

Love. Not sex but love. *Did she know anything about the word?* Because emotion ruled her, Melaine could do nothing less than stand and face him, the inches separating them all that stood between her and insanity. In a few, beautiful words he'd told her it was time for honesty. "Are we ready?" she had to ask. "There's so much—"

"I know. There's so much we haven't resolved." He took her hand, lifted it, touched his lips to her knuckles. Heat filled her like the tide washing over the shore.

"Things we might never resolve. But, Melaine, that's life. We all take it one day at a time. One issue at a time."

"But—"

"No. I don't want to hear it. Not tonight." Once again he brushed his lips over her flesh, and although she hadn't moved, she felt a bridging of the space between them. He laughed a little. "Cinderella and Prince Charming are the only people I know who walked off into the sunset, and my guess is, they didn't find happy-ever-after any more than the rest of us."

Tanner's wisdom brought a smile to Melaine's lips. "In-law problems. I imagine the prince had his hands full with Cinderella's relatives."

"And there must have been issues in the kingdom that took the prince from Cinderella's side. Civil unrest, financing for the army, natural disasters. Someone had to pick up the tab for the ball. Maybe there wasn't enough money in the coffers to cover it."

Melaine wound her fingers through Tanner's, laughing. "Could be Cinderella had to take a job to pay for future balls."

"Have you seen pictures of the prince? His orthodontist bills must have rivaled the national debt."

"Any man that good-looking had to be self-centered."

"And any girl who'd spent half her life cleaning the floor probably had a lot to learn about etiquette. The society matrons would have torn her apart." A look of horror twisted Tanner's features. "Do you think they really made a go of it? Maybe they wound up on 'Divorce Court.'"

"The prince would have never admitted he'd screwed up. He probably hired a shrink to try to straighten out Cinderella."

"While he went trapsing off with the ladies in waiting."

"The slime!" Melaine tried to look horrified but wound up giggling instead. "Do you have any idea what this has done to my belief in fairy tales? I'm devastated."

"I know what your childhood was like, Melaine. You don't believe in fairy tales."

Maybe not, but what was happening right now came as close as she'd ever wanted. Still smiling, Tanner drew her against him, his fingers gentle on her chin as he tilted her face upward. His eyes asked the question.

With her body, she gave him the only answer she had in her.

One day at a time. One moment at a time.

One more night of magic.

She felt his breath on her cheek, her lips, her throat. "I want to make love to you," he whispered.

"Yes." The word quavered; Melaine tried again. "Yes. I understand."

"I have to know how you feel."

Terrified. Starving. "You're the only man. Except for Chris, you're the only man I've ever made love to."

"I wish I'd known."

"I wish I'd told you. So many things I wish I'd told you."

His arms as strong as the cable that bore skiers to the top of a mountain, Tanner drew her into him until she felt nothing except his strength. Nothing in her held back, nothing asked to remain free. "We can begin tonight," he told her.

"Tonight." Trembling from something that felt a world away from weakness, Melaine looked up. His features blurred, but she remembered black hair, gray eyes, strength, and humor. He'd asked her a question that demanded the most honest answer she had in her. And, although she still caught glimpses of the chasm which existed between them, she knew what they both needed, and deserved to hear.

"I want you to stay the night," she told him.

"Not to talk. I don't want to talk."

"Neither do I."

How does a woman go about letting a man know she

wants to make love? The issue had never come up between her and Chris. The man wanted; he took; she allowed it to happen. Sometimes, in the beginning, she'd wanted it, too, but that had been so long ago that all she had was the whisper of a memory. Once she and Tanner had come together out of desperation and wonder.

Tonight she needed to understand. To give in to desire. To tap the woman in her.

Although she didn't possess the words to tell Tanner that, there was another way. Growing bold, or perhaps pushed by the pulsing need inside, Melaine reached for him. She ran her hands over his throat, her palms pressing past his shirt until she felt the hard ridge of his shoulder blade. He looked down at her, eyes hooded, his hands gripping her waist. Letting her begin the exploration.

His shirt buttons gave easily, unveiling a sprinkling of dark hair like spun wool. His flesh was satin, the muscle beneath an echo of the mountain which had brought both of them here. She pressed the tips of her fingers against his skin until the strength in him flooded through her, filling her with raw power. Groaning, Melaine lowered her head and ran her tongue and mouth over his throat, down to his chest, circling the hard and waiting nubs of his breasts. She felt him shudder and answered with a convulsive movement of her own.

As a teenager she'd read, not juvenile romances but about the man raised by jungle apes who ruled his savage world with physical strength. Tanner wasn't the mythical Tarzan. But tonight she could tap into the primitive appeal of a larger than life man who knew neither fear nor defeat.

Tanner was her strength. Her energy.

Unnerved by the thought, Melaine ran her cheek over Tanner's chest. What wisdom, what courage had brought them together tonight? She felt reckless and insane. They had no business doing this. He might believe that life could only be taken one step at a time, but wise and civilized people didn't play with fire.

She could be burned. They could both become scarred by this daring adventure.

But her fingers and cheek and heart absorbed him, and she became willing to take the risk.

With fingers that might have always known what he would feel like, Melaine tugged his shirt out of his waistband and pushed it off his shoulders. He stood in front of her, his eyes darker than the bottom of Lake Mary at midnight. If she dove into those eyes, she might drown.

But if she didn't, she might never learn to swim.

"My turn," Tanner whispered when, with nerve-filled fingers, she reached for the button at the top of his jeans. Gently, oh so gently, he pulled her hands free and placed them on his shoulders. His eyes still swimming in midnight, he looked down at her and made her feel as if she'd been born for this moment.

This man.

He kissed her chin, her throat, her eyelid. His warm, damp tongue found the pulse point at the side of her throat. She had to dig her fingers into his flesh to keep from swaying. Chris had never tapped this primitive creature inside her. And the one time she and Tanner had come together, she'd been so wounded that she'd buried herself in him without trying to understand why.

Now she stood before him, a woman. A woman who understood that promise could become reality.

Make love to me. Take me through the night. Show me—everything. Let me give you—everything.

And we won't talk about tomorrow.

Or us.

Without her caring how it happened, Tanner had stripped her of the prison of her sweater. Now her bra was in his hands; now it drifted downward to join that other discarded garment. They'd left on the lamp near the sliding-glass door. The lighting was more mood than reality. Still, she knew he could see enough of her that there could be no secrets. Her breasts weren't the perfect orbs of a model. But he'd done incredible things to her senses and nerves. Her nipples had hardened, thrusting toward him. They belonged to him.

With his weather-painted hands, he pressed against her rib cage and upward, bringing her breasts within reach of his lips. Slowly, so slowly that she nearly screamed with the waiting, he touched, tasted, covered. She felt the giving up of herself and nearly cried from wonder.

A sense of weight coiled through her, starting deep in her belly and spiraling downward. Whether his eyes remained bathed in midnight no longer mattered. Whether he found anything lacking about her body wasn't important. Only the lightning coursing through her felt real.

"Melaine? Melaine? It's going to be all right for you?"

"All right?"

"Safe?"

Oh Lord, he thought that much of her! "Yes. I—I have problems with my periods. I'm on the pill—to make them regular."

His breath filtered across her throat. "Good. I didn't plan this—happening. I didn't make any kind of preparations."

"I didn't plan it, either," she told him and then, because she needed to show him her strength, she cupped his head in her hands and drew his mouth back to her breasts. Fire danced through her.

"I can't— I don't want—" he stammered.

"Now. Please now."

She fit in his arms. Maybe she should have known that, but such an essential question could have been answered only by a woman with the ability to reason. Melaine had lost that ability. Instead, she had to experience being carried up the stairs and into the bedroom to know he could do it.

She had to feel his hands on her waist and pushing away the prison of her slacks to know.

And she had to fasten her fingers over his zipper to know she was capable of that bold and brazen behavior.

Because she hadn't heated the bedroom, the sheets felt cold. Melaine shivered, but a moment later Tanner joined her and chill turned into heat.

"The night," he rasped. "We have the night."

"Don't." Her voice carried a message of needs out of control. "I can't wait the night."

"This won't be the only time," he whispered, hands tracing the curve from hip to thigh.

Please. Let me believe that. Melaine covered his hand with hers, not to stop him, but in silent approval. Then, because knowing him meant that much to her, she touched the hard curve of his hipbone and inched inward. She buried her fingers in the forest of hair and found— No. There wouldn't be any waiting.

He wanted her.

Now.

Guiding both of them with reckless courage, Melaine eased onto her back. She reached for him, but he was already there. Over her.

Finding her.

Taking her into midnight and showing her that, tonight, there was nothing to fear.

TEN

Tanner's beeper went off at 6:10 A.M. He sat upright and groped around for his jeans. Then he hurried into the kitchen and picked up the phone. Melaine heard him speaking but couldn't make out his words.

He returned to the bedroom and sat on the side of the bed so he could lean over and kiss her. "Lousy timing," he whispered. "Try to get a little more rest." Before she had a chance to prepare for the loss, he left her. She stared after him as he headed into the bathroom. She tried to recapture the oblivion of sleep, but without him to share the bed with, it didn't matter.

"Problems?" she asked after throwing a robe over her shoulders and joining him in the bathroom.

He spoke from the shower. "I hope nothing serious. The chair at Milk Run isn't working. They're going to be routing people to Shaft. It's going to cause overcrowding, which means I'll have to do a little juggling of my men. I've got a fair idea what's wrong with the chair. If we can get it going—"

"Can I do anything to help?" Melaine asked, resisting the urge to wipe away the steam that fogged the door between them.

"Coffee."

She smiled. "Coffee it is. Do you often get called out of bed like that?"

"I don't usually have compelling reasons to stay in bed. Melaine?"

Something about Tanner's tone made her feel uneasy. "What?"

"We need to talk about last night. Think about it and then talk about it."

Hearing Tanner say the words cemented what had been swirling around her. She didn't need to look in the mirror to know she carried the marks of a woman who'd spent the night making love. She felt her swollen lips, cheeks roughened by his beard, the tenderness in her body. But those physical reminders would fade. What wouldn't was the necessary question of whether they'd let need come between them and wisdom. *One day at a time*, Tanner had prompted before taking her—before she'd taken him.

But were they ready for the next day?

"This isn't the time," she told him, and left the bathroom for the kitchen. She'd just poured coffee when Tanner emerged. Because he hadn't known he'd be spending the night, he wore what she'd stripped off him. That now seemed a lifetime ago.

Tanner wrapped his hands around the mug she gave him and held it close to his face while he explained that he intended to run by his place to change before heading for Milk Run. "You have to get going yourself pretty soon, don't you?" he asked.

Melaine glanced at the kitchen clock. Time still hadn't regained its importance in her life. Even with her hair tangled around her and the scent of steam and soap clinging to Tanner, part of her remained in the past. The innocent and unreal night. "Pretty soon. Will you have time for breakfast?"

"I'm not sure. Toast. I'll have that and juice."

As if it mattered, Melaine nodded. She knew she was putting off having to face what he'd said in the bathroom, but she also knew she couldn't do that until she'd gathered her courage around her. "Let me know, will you? I'll be curious to learn how things turn out."

"I will. Melaine. About—"

"No. Not yet. I need coffee and a shower."

"You don't know what I'm going to say."

"Don't I?" Melaine asked, and let him go.

From what she heard, the problem with the chair was more complicated than anyone had anticipated. The patrol member who dropped by the clinic a little before noon explained that Tanner had worked with the mechanic for about an hour before leaving to take a look at a spot particularly susceptible to avalanches. The area had been cordoned off and the necessary blasting had already taken place. Now man and machine were at work so skiers could use the area again. The lift was still inoperable.

Despite being concerned that Tanner was trying to accomplish too much, Melaine was glad for the reprieve. As the hours slipped away, she regained her sense of reality. The phone rang. People limped or hobbled into the clinic. She spoke via the CB to rangers and patrol members. Carol dropped by for a quick checkup. Keeping busy didn't give her much time to think. True, her body remembered. True, just hearing Tanner's name made her feel lightheaded, but at least she wasn't being asked to confront the most impossible of questions.

Were they both insane for having spent last night lost in each other?

She answered that question at Tanner's place after work. She hadn't intended to stop, but he was outside working on his truck as she came along the narrow lake road. He nodded when she pulled up beside his vehicle. He smiled, but the gesture ended before reaching his eyes. "I'm sorry," he said over the sound of his idling engine. "There was just no way I could get away during the day. I was going to see or at least call you tonight, only—"

Shaking his head, he glared at the open hood. "A classic example of the mechanic who doesn't have time to tend to his own vehicle. Hopefully, flushing out the radiator will take care of things."

Melaine couldn't pretend she cared about what was wrong with Tanner's truck. Still, she waited patiently while he worked on it for another five minutes. Finally he reached in the cab and turned the key. In the silence that followed, she felt the world beyond the two of them fade away. In a few minutes it would be night. For the first time since snow began falling last week, the sky was clear. She hoped the moon would be out.

The moon might keep night from surrounding her.

"You said we had to talk," she said as he wiped his hands on a rag.

"Inside. I don't want you getting cold."

Thanks to the local stores, Melaine now had proper winter wear. But what Tanner said made sense. They needed to work certain things out. They didn't have to do it standing outside.

Tanner's house had lost its mountain air smell, but she didn't mind the change. Now she caught the subtle scent of wood heat and felt herself being drawn to the well-stoked cast-iron stove. Tanner disappeared into the kitchen and Melaine pulled off her coat. She didn't bother loosening the ties on her boots. Somehow she knew she wouldn't be staying long.

He returned with two heavy pottery mugs. "Hot chocolate," he said. "I started the water heating before I went outside. The earth's dancing again. I didn't want anyone telling you that over the CB. I was afraid a skier would pick that up and jump to a lot of conclusions."

Melaine turned her back to the stove, watching as Tanner ran his fingers over the tiny imperfections on his handmade cup. She almost made the mistake of asking him who the potter was, but that might distract them from what needed to be said.

She wished she wasn't a mature professional. If she was a child, she could run from this hard yet necessary conversation. "The tremors, are they anything we should be worried about?"

"Who knows? Mother Nature does what she's going to do. Melaine, I'm sorry."

"Sorry?"

"That last night happened."

Despite his words, Melaine accepted them without anger. He wasn't a man to mince words. What he believed, he said. And she had to know what was going on inside him.

"I think maybe I'm sorry, too," she told him while her traitor's body screamed a silent and primitive denial. "We talked about how we live in the real world and can't wait for the fairy tale to begin."

"I believe that. I always will," he said. "But I think I lost sight of what that real world stands for."

Hating herself for having to do it, Melaine nodded. "We haven't resolved the most important thing, have we?"

"No." He lifted the mug to his lips, swallowed, then touched her with a haunting smile. "Chris is still part of your life."

"This isn't about Chris."

"No," he conceded. "It isn't. But he makes a better scapegoat than a little girl."

An innocent little girl. He'd acknowledged what Amber was. "Is that how you see her? A scapegoat?"

"No. It's a hell of a lot more complicated than that."

"Yes it is." The heat radiating from the wood stove felt comforting. Although she wanted to be farther away from Tanner so she could avoid his impact, she remained where she was. "I can't do it, Tanner. No matter what you think, no matter what arguments you come up with, I can't walk out of her life."

Melaine couldn't call his straightforward gaze a glare.

She felt as if he was trying to reach into her innermost core, trying to understand the forces operating within her. The way he held himself, half reaching, half holding back, told him he did understand.

But enough?

She tried again. "It isn't her versus you. What I'm experiencing isn't as simple as that."

"I know."

"I can't say that what I feel for her goes beyond what I feel for you. They—the emotions—are so different."

"I'm an adult. She's a child."

"I look at you and I feel—attraction." *Only attraction? Wasn't she capable of more?* "I think I understand a woman's needs for a man in her life. And then I look at Amber and feel something so basic that maybe the emotion doesn't have words."

"You love her."

His words almost doubled her over. "Y-es."

"Even though that love might keep you from experiencing what else life has to offer."

Melaine turned away. They'd been through this before. She knew what he was trying to say. Only . . . Life without Amber?

Life without Tanner?

Was he asking her to make that choice?

Why? It wasn't as if they loved each other. Certainly not that.

Suddenly an image of her parents flashed through her mind. She shook off the thought, but it came back. She remembered so little of her father—a dark-haired, gray-eyed man who seldom spoke. The memory of her mother was stronger—lines around her mouth, a body so angular that a child couldn't cuddle up against it.

"Tell me something," Melaine managed while tears boiled inside her. "Are you saying there can't be anything between us as long as I try to be a mother to Amber?"

Although she resisted, Tanner turned her back around.

"You aren't her mother, Melaine. And, no. I'd never ask you to chose between us. Damn it, I hope you know me better than that. But I said it before. I still believe it. You've put your life on hold because of her. I'm not sure there's enough of you left over to explore another kind of relationship."

He thought— Melaine opened her mouth to tell him he had no idea what he was talking about, that he had no right proclaiming himself the expert where her heart and mind were concerned.

But maybe he was right. She'd been divorced three years, and except for Tanner, there hadn't been a man in her life. She hadn't wanted one.

And she'd done everything within her power to land a job that would bring her close to Amber.

Her head pounding, Melaine concentrated on her chocolate. She wanted the hot liquid to have the power to wash away the feeling that she'd never be anything but what she was tonight—a woman alone.

"I can't live your life for you, Melaine." His voice, growling with something he'd chosen to keep to himself, filled her senses. "Something happens when we're together. Last night showed me that."

It did.

"But sleeping together isn't enough."

Melaine filled her lungs once, twice. It didn't help. She wanted to cry. She needed to cry.

"No." She reached for her coat. "It isn't. You deserve more."

"Me?" He took the cup from her and stepped back so he wouldn't stand between her and the door. "You're the one who deserves more."

Tanner waited until Melaine had driven away before carrying the mugs into the kitchen. He reached for the refrigerator door, opened it, and stared at its contents.

Although he'd missed lunch and attributed his headache to an empty stomach, he couldn't concentrate on food.

His thoughts followed Melaine home. He pictured her making her way up her recently shoveled steps, pulling out her keys, unlocking the door. She'd step inside and switch on the lamp that had painted last night in soft light. After turning up the heat, she'd walk up the steps and into her bedroom.

Had she made her bed? Did it still carry his imprint? If so, how would she react? Would her image of him be strong enough to take her thoughts from the other person in her life? Or would Amber win?

Tanner balled his hand into a fist. No, damn it. This wasn't a matter of winning or losing. He wasn't in competition with the girl for Melaine's affection. He wasn't that self-centered, that immature. But if he didn't try to make Melaine understand that she couldn't remain in limbo, waiting for some impossible fairy tale to come true, who would play that role?

The way he saw it, the only way he could possibly see it, was that Melaine had sentenced herself to a half life. He wanted her to be free from that. For her sake. And, damn it, for his.

Only, he had no idea how to make her see that. Or how she'd survive that painful decision.

ELEVEN

Tanner called the next morning to tell her he'd be spending the next two days at June Mountain. "I don't know where we're heading," he said once the specifics of his trip were over. "I don't think either of us does. But maybe we need a couple of days apart."

"Maybe we do."

"Only, when I get back, we're going to have to talk again."

Melaine sighed. She hadn't cried when she left Tanner, but the unspent tears had never quite left her. She spoke around them. "I don't know what good that's going to do."

"Anything has to be better than saying nothing. We're so far from a resolution, and yet there has to be one. Melaine, I want to try to help you get through this."

As long as I see it your way, she thought. Although his being gone would leave a void, in a way she was grateful. A few days alone with her thoughts would help. Surely by the time he returned, she'd understand her emotions. She'd be able to tell him—

Only, the next time she heard a male voice on her home phone, it wasn't Tanner.

"We just drove into town," Chris said on Thursday evening. "We've checked into the Skylight Chateau. If you'd like to join us for dinner—"

"You're in Mammoth? What are you doing here?"

"Business. I wasn't going to haul Amber with me, but she insisted. Look, we're going to eat in about an hour. If you and what's his name—the man Amber told me about—feel like it . . ."

Did she want Tanner to be part of this? Before she'd climbed halfway up her stairs, Melaine had her answer. It would be easier if she didn't have to weather an uncomfortable meeting between Chris and Tanner, but there was so much Tanner didn't understand. He couldn't possibly see what kind of relationship Chris and Amber had unless he observed Chris's distance, his lack of response, firsthand. By the end of the evening surely Tanner would realize that while Chris provided well financially for his daughter, there were other things—things like spontaneous displays of love that Chris simply wasn't capable of.

Those things, if Amber was going to go on experiencing them, had to come from her.

Tanner, who'd just gotten back from June Mountain, admitted he didn't know what to make of the invitation. "It sounds like the kind of fun I can pass on. Don't the three of you need some time together?"

"We had time," Melaine pointed out. "Years. It didn't do any good. Please, Tanner, you said you want to understand what I'm going through. How can you if you don't even know the man?"

"He wants this?"

"He says he does. He—well, he doesn't know how it is for us."

"How *is* it for us, Melaine?"

Tanner had asked the hardest question of all, but she didn't expect him to do otherwise. "I don't have the answer to that," she told him. "But I can't even try tonight. Will you join us?"

"Yeah."

Chris and Amber were already seated in the enormous dining room when Melaine arrived. For a moment she stared at them, hurting as she always did when she thought of Chris and Amber together without her. She'd tried to call Amber last night, but the girl had been at a friend's house. She'd felt both let down and delighted because she was spending time with a friend. Maybe that's what they'd talk about. That way Chris might understand that his daughter needed more than a housekeeper. Melaine squared her shoulders but glanced behind her before taking that first step.

The front door opened, and Tanner walked inside. Acknowledging her, he placed his arm around her shoulder. "How are you holding up?" he whispered.

"Nervous," Melaine admitted, resting her head against him momentarily. He could have said a thousand things, and as long as she heard his voice, she'd respond. But he'd asked about her emotional state and that meant more than anything else could. Had it only been two days since she'd seen him? It seemed forever.

"I'll try to remember my manners. And I promise not to deck him, unless I have good cause. Will that help?"

Melaine gave him a fleeting smile. "It might. I don't know how Amber's going to handle this."

"Why don't you worry about yourself. Amber has her own agenda."

Melaine almost pointed out that Amber was a child and had no control over the situation. However, there wasn't time to go into a long explanation about how children acted and reacted. "She loves going out to eat," Melaine said as they started toward Chris's table. "She orders things she's never heard of. Sometimes she likes them and sometimes . . ." Chris turned toward them; Melaine's words trailed off.

The act of introducing Tanner and Chris turned her stomach into a thousand knots. What were the guidelines?

"Tanner, I'd like you to meet the man I couldn't stay married to. Chris, I'd like you to say hello to the man who drives me crazy."

Wonderful.

"So you're the one who keeps this place working smoothly, are you?" Chris asked as the men shook hands. "Amber told me you're a . . . what'd she call it—an awesome skier."

Tanner winked at Amber, who was folding and refolding her napkin, and sat down. "I appreciate the compliment. To set the record straight, I'm hardly the brains behind the operation. My concern is with safety. Other considerations, particularly financial, are, thank heavens, on other shoulders."

"Tell me about it." Chris's groan sounded authentic. "Having the buck stop with me is going to give me ulcers. Fortunately, I seem to thrive on pressure."

While Melaine fought the demons in her stomach and tried to catch Amber's attention, Chris and Tanner carried on a spirited conversation about their various areas of responsibility. Before they'd been talking a minute, they found a common thread. Tanner dealt with physical safety while Chris was concerned with keeping a business operating in the black. Still, the bottom line was that the quality of the lives of those they dealt with depended on how well the two men did their jobs.

"Maybe we ought to switch," Chris said. He lifted his hand to signal the waiter. "A day in each other's shoes would probably make us grateful we've each found our own niche."

"Probably," Tanner agreed. When the waiter arrived, Tanner consulted Chris and then ordered two beers. He asked Melaine if she wanted a glass of wine. She declined, as did Amber when Tanner suggested a Shirley Temple.

"I thought you liked fruit drinks," Melaine said. "Are you sure?"

Amber shook her head. Occasionally she focused on her

father, but for the most part she seemed locked in her own world. Her miserable world.

Melaine didn't try to follow the threads of the conversation between Tanner and Chris. Obviously they were perfectly capable of carrying on without her. She tried to ask Amber about the friend she'd gone to see, but the girl answered in monosyllables.

"Is she all right?" she asked Chris. "Are you sure she's not getting sick?"

Chris shot his daughter a quick look. "She's pouting. Tripping over her lower lip."

"What about?" If Amber and Chris were at loggerheads about something, this wasn't the best time to bring it up. But she couldn't concentrate on anything except Amber's obvious misery.

"She's a child, Melaine. She doesn't understand that sometimes I have to do things she doesn't like."

"What kind of things?"

For a moment Melaine wasn't sure Chris was going to answer. He took a swallow of the beer the waiter had just delivered, then met her eyes, briefly.

"Details. Complications. We're going to be moving."

Melaine felt physically ill. "Moving?"

"To Aspen."

For a moment she could only stare as the word sunk in. "No," she stammered. "No. You just moved—"

"I know. And I'm probably going to lose money initially. But the business is really taking off in Aspen. I'm pretty much the local whiz kid with the monied skiing set there. I need to capitalize on that."

"Aspen," Melaine stammered. "No."

Chris turned toward Tanner. "Explain it to her, will you? I'm in a cutthroat business. The competition is incredible. I can't compete long distance." He reached out to pat his daughter's head, but Amber shied away. Chris's features clouded. "She'll adjust. The glitz and glamour are a little heavy, but it's a beautiful place, and they have child-care centers that take kids all hours of the day and night."

"I want to stay here," Amber moaned. "I want to be near Melaine!"

Melaine couldn't speak. She still felt as if she'd been shot. She sensed Tanner's eyes on her but didn't trust herself to look at him. Amber gone? No!

"Amber doesn't give a damn about child-care centers."

Tanner's clipped tones caught Melaine's attention. She shot him a quick look, shocked at the tension radiating from him. If he said something to antagonize Chris . . .

"Maybe she doesn't," Chris rejoined. "But it's a necessary issue. I have incredible demands on my time, and I can't do my job if I'm always having to juggle Amber around."

"She could be with me." Melaine wasn't sure she'd spoken aloud. When both men turned toward her, she knew. "You know how I—"

"I know," Chris interrupted. "Melaine, we've been over this a hundred times. Amber is my child. Look . . ." Chris leaned forward his gaze intense. "I know you won't agree, but I've given this a lot of thought. Amber was just getting into a routine before you moved to Mammoth. Now all she talks about is coming to visit you, her room here, helping you at the clinic. Being torn between two places isn't good for her."

Not good for her? How could Chris believe that? Tanner gripped her hand. She squeezed back, but couldn't tear her eyes from Chris. "How could you say that?" she managed, her head pounding. "Chris, Amber needs a woman in her life. A mother figure. I fill that role."

"Thousands of kids have survived without one. Look, I didn't want to get into this now, but if you insist . . ." Chris glanced at Tanner, then down at the intertwined hands. When he spoke again, his voice had lost its emotional tone and become the cool, in-control one Melaine knew all too well. "Things have changed for you, Melaine. I've worried about you. I know you find that hard to believe, but I really have. You're the kind of woman who needs to feel needed. For too long all there was was Amber. But you have someone else now." He indicated Tanner. "Amber has me, as it should be. You have Tanner. Let it go."

Let Amber go? Never. Not as long as she lived. "She's just starting to make friends in Bishop. You don't understand what this is going to do to her," Melaine whispered. With her free hand, she reached for Amber, hating the tears streaming down the girl's cheeks.

"Just as you don't understand where I'm coming from. Do you want me to say it again? I'm Amber's parent. Me. Not you. She'll make new friends."

Shaking, Melaine pulled free from Tanner and turned to grip Amber more tightly. Amber's body convulsed, and she gripped Melaine with incredible strength. How could Chris do this to her? To his daughter! He didn't understand. God, he'd never understand! "Aspen," she whispered. "You're moving to Aspen."

Until Melaine's agony washed through him, Tanner had been trying to convince himself that he was nothing more than an unwilling bystander. Damn it, if he'd known the evening was going to turn out this way, he would have never agreed to join them.

Right, he berated himself. *Like you don't care.*

"Look, Chris, you've dropped a bomb tonight. One Melaine didn't expect, and one that's got Amber pretty upset. Why don't we give them a few minutes. In the meantime . . ." Not really sure where in the hell he was taking the conversation, Tanner got to his feet and stared pointedly at Chris. The man wasn't a pretty boy. Why did he feel like rearranging his face? "In the meantime, why don't you and I go for a walk."

Chris's look said he was sizing up the situation, and coming up with the short straw. Tanner couldn't remember the last time he'd used his physical size to control a situation—certainly not since high school. Tonight, being over six feet with muscles honed by a physical life served him in good stead. He spread his legs just slightly, his hands hanging not quite easily by his side. He lifted his chin and looked down, daring Chris to turn him down.

After a quick blink that gave away his nervousness, Chris stood. "I don't know what you want to prove—"

"I'm not trying to prove anything. But your daughter's already in tears. I'd prefer we speak in private."

Neither man spoke until they were outside. Tanner remembered Melaine's stricken, panicked eyes, but she hadn't tried to stop him. Instead she'd kept her arms tightly around Amber, her own face chalk-white. If she'd begged him to stay inside the restaurant, out of consideration for her, he probably would have dropped his half-baked plan to have a man-to-man talk with Chris.

"Your timing sucked."

Chris stiffened. "The timing would have never been right as far as she's concerned. And Amber's been crying since I told her. I thought Aspen would excite her, but no. All she thinks about is leaving Melaine. Look, Tanner, you haven't known Melaine as long as I have. She's a competent, intelligent woman. I'll never argue that. But she's got this fixation on Amber. It's got the girl so turned around—"

"It's called love."

Chris shrugged. The gesture told Tanner more than he wanted to know about the other man's makeup.

"The reason I wanted to talk to you out here," Tanner said when Chris remained silent, "is to try to get something straight in my head. Melaine told me she asked you to give her custody of Amber."

Chris grunted. "More times than I want to think about."

"What did you think?"

"What do you mean, what did I think?"

"I mean . . ." Damn it. Was he going about this right,

or would what he was trying to say backfire in Melaine's face? He'd do anything to prevent that. And yet he could do nothing. "Listening to you back in there, I got the distinct impression that making your business succeed, putting it into high gear, is the most important thing in your life. At least the most time consuming. I have to hand it to you. There aren't many small businesses that make it. Doing that while being a single parent—it's damn hard."

"Tell me about it."

"Melaine would make a good mother. I've seen her and Amber together. It doesn't take a genius to see the love between them."

"Yeah. Melaine's all but lived in Amber's pocket. And Amber would be calling her Mother if I'd let her."

That comment set Tanner's teeth on edge, but he didn't dare let it distract him from what he believed he needed to say. "They'd be good together. Maybe Melaine isn't her biological mother, but I don't think that matters. Amber needs a mother, and Melaine has been doing everything she can to fill that role."

"Look . . ." Chris balled his hands into fists. "I told you. I've already heard this from Melaine."

"Then why don't you let her?" Tanner asked, the question rolling out of him.

"Why don't I let Melaine have custody of Amber?"

"Yeah."

"Do you really think I could do that and face myself?"

Chris's question struck a harsh cord with Tanner. It took a moment for him to filter through to the why. Chris hadn't said anything about loving Amber too much to let her go. "Face yourself," Tanner pressed. "What do you mean?"

"Are your folks alive?"

"What? Yes. Why?"

"Mine, too," Chris said, and folded his arms across his chest. He shivered in the night air and pressed his arms tightly against his body. "My father's a millionaire. Did Melaine tell you that?"

If she had, Tanner didn't remember. "What does he do?"

"Investments. The man knows the stock market . . . That's not the point. The point is, it hasn't been easy living up to his expectations. His or my mother's."

Tanner hadn't thought about that. As a small boy, he'd fantasized about what he'd do and buy if his parents were rich; it had been a long time since money meant that much to him. But if Chris's father was a self-made millionaire, maybe he put pressure on his son to follow in his footsteps. "You're not interested in the stock market?"

"I could never duplicate my old man's success. I've always known that I had to make it on my own. And I'm doing it." Chris's voice took on a note of defiance and pride. "I'm not a millionaire yet, but I'm on my way. A few more years . . . They're proud of me. I want you to know that. They're proud of what I've accomplished."

"I'm glad," Tanner said, and then shut up, waiting for Chris to continue.

"My folks have never been the kind to gush affection. It isn't part of their makeup. Mine, either." He glanced toward the restaurant door. "Amber, she's my responsibility. Mine. What would my folks think if I turned my back on that?"

Chris hadn't said anything about grandparents' love for their grandchild. In fact, Tanner couldn't remember Melaine saying anything about Chris's parents role in Amber's life. Chris had just called his daughter a responsibility. Was that how all of them viewed an eight-year-old girl?

"You won't give Melaine custody of Amber because she's your obligation?"

"Look, Tanner, my parents made sure I got the best education possible. If it wasn't for them, I wouldn't know the first thing about making a business succeed. A pragmatic nature is essential in today's world. I can't do anything less for my daughter than instill in her the necessary skills to succeed. I will not turn my back on her."

"Even if that means uprooting her from the only mother she's ever known?"

Chris stiffened. "She's my daughter, Tanner. My obligation, as you call it. Only, I can't put my career on hold because she wants to stay here. She'll survive. Just as, now that she's got you, so will Melaine."

Melaine didn't want to think about what might be going on between Tanner and Chris. Still, the state of her stomach told her she'd failed. Miserably. She tried to talk to Amber, but the girl was so upset. She couldn't think of any words that wouldn't reduce both of them to more tears. Her brain felt like a wild animal, racing from one side of a trap to another, seeking a way out. Finding none.

"I don't want to go with him!" Amber moaned. "Daddy's going to be gone all the time. He's always gone. Can't I stay with you?"

"Oh, honey!" Melaine tried to close her ears to the sound of her heart breaking. "You know there's nothing I want more. But he's your father."

"I wish you were my mommy."

Melaine swallowed. The waiter hovered nearby. Couldn't he tell that food was the last thing on either of their minds? Irrationally, she wanted to scream at the young man, make him understand that, once again, her world had shattered.

But he was just trying to do his job.

"Damn cold out there. Why I don't design surfboards and live in San Diego I'll never know."

Melaine forced herself to look up. Chris's nose had turned red, and he was shivering, but she didn't care. His eyes told her nothing of what was going on inside him, but then they seldom did. She turned toward Tanner. The man was a study in caged energy, impotent fury struggling to escape. He hadn't hit Chris. That's all she could think about. At least he'd remained that civilized.

Tanner lowered himself into his chair, but ignored the beer at his elbow. He stared at her, his eyes shading into black and boiling with emotion.

For at least a full minute, no one spoke. Accustomed to trying to placate Chris, Melaine searched her mind for the necessary words, but he'd rubbed her raw. The only thing she could concentrate on was Amber. And heartache.

And the flutterings of an insane, desperate plan.

"I take it no one's in the mood for dinner," Chris said at last. "Look, I would have preferred to wait until later to make my announcement, but I'm not responsible for what comes out of my daughter's mouth." For the second time that evening, he tried to touch Amber. Again she jerked away. Chris's lips tightened; still, Melaine saw more confusion than anger in his eyes. "I thought this would be a good opportunity for the four of us to sit down together. Obviously, I was wrong. Melaine, if you want to leave—"

He was giving her permission? As if she needed that from him! But that wasn't the issue at all. Chris honestly thought she could ignore the agony in Amber's eyes and the pain in her own heart and walk out the door. After all these years, he still didn't understand. "What counts is what Amber wants." She forced out the words. "It's her life that's being disrupted."

"You have a point." Chris shifted his weight and turned toward Melaine. "In fact, that's one of the reasons I wanted to see you while I was here. I'm going to be pretty tied up over the next couple of weeks. Moving my operation. Finding a place to live. It'd be a lot simpler if I didn't have to worry about Amber."

Did he want Amber to stay with her? Clinging to that lifeline, Melaine waited.

"It's up to you, of course," Chris said calmly. "If it gets in the way of your plans . . . I thought it would give you time to talk to her. Make her understand that I really have no choice."

"You want Melaine to keep Amber for two weeks and then turn her over to you? You bas— You really don't get it, do you!"

Tanner's hostility lashed around Melaine. Her body trembling with tension, she turned on him. "Tanner. Don't. You don't—"

"Don't what?" Tanner demanded. "Don't say anything to upset Chris? He might take back his 'generous' offer. Might haul Amber off with him."

He might. It wouldn't be the first time he's used her. "I want her with me," Melaine managed. "There's never been any question of that."

"Do you think I don't know that?" Although he remained tense, Melaine sensed that Tanner was struggling to get his emotions under control. "Say it, Melaine," he whispered. "You want me to stay out of this."

"I—want Amber."

"No matter what it does to your heart when you have to give her up."

Melaine could only nod. Two weeks. She was being given Amber for two weeks.

Even if that meant losing Tanner?

Tanner turned on Chris. "I'm not going to say what I think in front of your daughter. She deserves better than that. But I can't believe you're going to put her and Melaine through hell simply because it solves a problem for you. They're going to spend two weeks together knowing it can't last. Scared to death of each hour which brings them closer to the end. Didn't it occur to you that it'd be easier on them if you just made the break clean? No. Of course not." Tanner half rose, his bulk seeming to fill the room. "You aren't capable of thinking that way, are you?"

"Tanner." Melaine found her voice. Only, just one word came out. "Tanner."

"No," he told her. "I'm not going to butt out. Maybe I'm the only one who can look at this objectively. Melaine, I don't want to see your heart broken. Yours or Amber's. But that's what's going to happen if you agree to this insanity."

Insanity. Tanner was right. Something insane was taking place here. Melaine had no idea how it had begun. All she knew was that if Tanner said anything more, Chris would walk out the door—with Amber. "I want you to leave." Through misted eyes, she faced Tanner. "Now."

Tanner looked as if she'd struck him. But he didn't move. "Not without you."

"What?"

"You heard me! I'm not leaving without you."

Terrified that Tanner was losing his grip on his barely contained rage, Melaine had no choice but to do as he said. When she stood, her legs threatened to collapse. Still, she managed to walk over to Amber and hug her once more. "I know where you're staying," she whispered. "I'll come see you in the morning."

Amber looked up at her, her eyes too big, her face too pale. "Promise?"

"Promise."

"Put on your coat. We're going for a walk."

Dimly, Melaine wondered why she hadn't thought about bundling up herself, but with everything boiling inside her, she couldn't be expected to concentrate on something as unimportant as the elements. "You don't have any idea what you've done, do you?" she asked as he steered her down the street.

"I figure you'll tell me."

She would. Only, he was walking so close that it took a moment for her to learn how to deal with that. She wouldn't think about him. That's it. She'd simply say what she had to, what she dared. And she wouldn't think—about him.

"You almost called him a bastard."

"If Amber hadn't been there, I would have."

"You can't." Melaine stared ahead. She tried to think about drifting snowflakes catching the light prisms coming from streetlights. She tried not to think about the arm around her waist, or the way his hip kept kissing hers. "Chris believes he's right. He's always believed he's right. I learned never to forget that. As long as I agree with him as much as possible, he doesn't lock me out."

"Why should you care whether he locks you out of his life?"

"Not mine. Amber's. Don't you see?" Melaine risked a look at Tanner. The burnished overhead lights glittered in his eyes and, wisely, desperately, she looked away. "He knows you and I are seeing each other. I'm sure Amber has talked to him about you."

"So?"

"Tanner, he's a business success because he knows how to size up the opposition. He stands his ground. He doesn't back down."

"I'm not planning on getting in a boxing ring with him."

"Don't make fun of me." Melaine blinked away a snowflake that had landed on her lashes. Another touched her cheek. She tried to concentrate on the cold, but Tanner's arm kept her waist warm. Too warm. "No one crosses Chris. If he thinks that's happening, he goes on the attack."

"No wonder you divorced him."

Even though she agreed, that wasn't the point. "I learned to give in to him. Do you think I wanted to? Of course not. But if it meant holding on to Amber, I would do whatever he wanted. But you almost called him a bastard. You accused him of—a lot of things."

"I told him he was heartless. He is, you know."

Melaine did know. Although she usually managed to block that out, concentrating instead on the creature comforts he provided for his daughter, she'd lived with him long enough to know that something was missing from

Chris's makeup. Tanner might have said it all wrong, but he was right. Chris didn't think about other people's emotions because he didn't have that capacity. "He's letting Amber stay with me for two weeks."

"Melaine." Tanner stopped and turned her toward him so quickly that she didn't know what he'd done until it was too late. Now she had no choice but to look up at him. Accept his night-darkened eyes. "I didn't want to say what I did in front of Amber, and I don't want to do what I'm going to now, but if I don't, I'm afraid you won't see what you're letting yourself into. Right now the only thing you can think about is two weeks with Amber."

Melaine nodded and fought the emotion sweeping through her. Tanner. She needed Tanner.

"You won't let yourself face what it'll be like once she's gone."

Gone? No! "It doesn't have to be like that," she blurted. She wanted to cry. She wanted Tanner's arms around her and the world stripped away. Instead she voiced her desperate, insane thoughts. "I can move. To Aspen. They must need nurses. Chris won't refuse to let me see Amber. I'd be there whenever he needs someone to look after her. I—I'll find someone to take my place here." She winced as tears boiled over and seared her chilled cheeks. "I have to. Somehow I have to—"

"Melaine! Don't! You don't know what you're talking about."

Didn't she? With Tanner's arms around her, all she could do was think. And feel. About—everything and nothing. "Come there with me. We'll find a place. With your skills you—"

"I'm not moving to Aspen. And neither are you."

"No." Melaine wanted to wipe her tears away, but her arms had turned to lead. Just like her heart. "You can't mean that."

"I can. I have to. Melaine, you can't spend your life

running after Amber. Life. One of your own. That's what you deserve.''

Although she still needed him as maybe she'd never needed anything before in life, Melaine struggled free. She knew she couldn't have done that if Tanner had held on to her, but she couldn't concentrate on that. He'd said that wanting and needing Amber was unhealthy. He'd said he wouldn't go with her.

He'd left her with nothing.

TWELVE

"Can I wear a dress?"

Melaine turned from her study of the lake beyond the A-frame and looked at what Amber was holding. The yellow dress would have been more appropriate for summertime wear, but by next summer it probably wouldn't fit. Besides, in the past five days, Melaine hadn't been able to refuse Amber anything.

"I don't see why not. I'm sure Carol will have her wood stove going. This isn't going to be anything fancy, you know. Just some friends getting together."

"You said it was a party."

"It is. Sort of. Carol just wants everyone to share her joy at being pregnant. I think she's kind of gone off the deep end."

Amber wanted to know what going off the deep end meant. Melaine tried to explain by pointing out how excited Amber used to get at Christmas, but wasn't sure how successful she'd been. She could have reminded Amber of the night when she, Amber, Chris, and Tanner had tried to have dinner together. Tanner had gone off the deep end when he jumped on Chris, but that wasn't the point, either. If Amber had seen her desperate attempt to convince Tanner that they had to pull up stakes and move to Aspen, the girl would understand the term's true meaning.

Fortunately, Amber hadn't seen. And Melaine had put that insane thought behind her. Tanner had managed to reach through her panic and make her understand. She couldn't turn her back on the work she'd begun here. In truth, she didn't want that.

Just as she couldn't wipe Tanner from her life.

Even if she didn't understand what she felt around him, she didn't want that.

Knowing what would happen if she allowed her mind to begin running in that circle again, Melaine concentrated on helping Amber get ready. She had the girl for two weeks, minus five days. Every day, each minute was precious, and with a child's resiliency, Amber had regained her innate enthusiasm for life. True, she stuck closer than usual to Melaine and refused to talk about the future, but at least she'd begun smiling again. Maybe she believed Melaine capable of pulling off a miracle.

"I don't know about those," Melaine said when Amber reached for her new tennis shoes. "They really don't go with a dress."

"But I don't like my fancy shoes. They pinch my feet."

"That's because you're growing. I have something people spray on their shoes to get them to stretch. If that doesn't help, I guess everyone will just have to admire you in tennis shoes."

The spray did the work. Amber needed help fixing her hair and then insisted that Melaine put on a dress. "You do too have one," she protested when Melaine tried to beg off. "And you look really pretty in a dress."

Melaine didn't care about pretty. Even if Tanner showed up tonight, the two of them would have no more to say to each other than they had in the past five days. Still, to please Amber, she slipped into a slim, understated light-green dress she'd last worn during union negotiations in Sacramento. At Amber's insistence, she complemented it with a long gold necklace, and earrings that brushed against her neck every time she moved.

"Carol's going to think I'm putting on the dog," Melaine announced.

"What's putting on the dog?"

Melaine groaned. She had to stop using such phrases. Amber would only press for an explanation. Fortunately, that was easier to explain than the one about going off the deep end. Amber, ready and very much aware of how she looked, stood in a corner of the bathroom as Melaine applied makeup. Melaine had been content with a little powder and lipstick, but Amber wanted to see her with eye shadow. Impulsively, Melaine touched a dab of smoky-blue color to the outside of Amber's lids. "There. Now you're really going to knock the boys dead." She cringed. Would Amber ask for yet another explanation?

She didn't. "Do you think Tanner will like the way we look?"

Tanner. Tanner, with his hard and unwavering belief that she had to forge a life without Amber. "I don't know," she tried to sidestep. "I'm not sure he'll be there."

"I hope so. He made Daddy mad, you know. But he didn't really mean to."

"What makes you say that?"

"Because it wasn't like he was trying to pick a fight or anything. He didn't want to see you or me sad. He was just trying to help."

"Yes," Melaine admitted. "He was trying to help."

Amber's shoulders sagged. "But he couldn't, could he?"

"No. He couldn't."

"Because Daddy says I have to move with him. If you married Daddy again—"

"Amber," Melaine broke in. "You were very young when your Daddy and I were married. You don't remember that we didn't get along."

"But you get along now. No matter what Daddy says, you don't argue with him."

Was that how Amber saw it? The thought gave Melaine no sense of accomplishment. Instead she realized how much she'd compromised herself to accommodate Chris's value system. Oh, God, was Tanner right after all?

Because she was the only child there, Amber held back when they first arrived at the Edmondses' two story-house, but her touch of shyness didn't last long. Carol told Amber that Rabbit had missed her. The massive horse *needed* to be scratched behind her ears. A couple of carrots wouldn't hurt, either. After telling Melaine to hold down the fort, Carol put on a jacket and slipped out to the barn with Amber.

There wasn't much for Melaine to do. The dozen or so guests had been to the Edmondses' place enough that they knew how to fend for themselves. Conversation flowed from weather forecasts to the stunts some of the weekend warriors pulled. Determined to put at least a temporary end to her depression, Melaine joined in with a few stories of her own about desk jockeys who like to think of themselves as mountain men and wound up barely able to get out of bed the next morning.

Tanner wasn't there.

Amber returned full of talk about Rabbit and the other horses. She was going to buy a horse herself, just as soon as she'd figured out where to keep it. She didn't want to hurt Carol's feelings, but her steed was going to be fast instead of strong. The fastest horse in the world.

Melaine handed Amber a paper plate with a hot dog on it that she'd decorated with catsup and no onions, just the way Amber liked it. "If you're going to get the fastest horse in the world, you'd better be strong enough to ride it," she pointed out. "Eat. You can talk later."

Amber bit into her bun. "Carol says she's going to give one of her horses to Tanner because she can't get it to do what he's supposed to, and Tanner wants to hitch it to a snowplow. Where is he? Bert said he's going to be here."

Melaine didn't have an answer. She really should have asked about Tanner, but it had been nearly impossible to speak his name. Maybe if he'd had some contact with her since the night he and Chris met . . .

Why did she have to look so much like a woman?

Tanner stopped at the entrance to the living room, his eyes zeroed in on Melaine in a roomful of people. He'd come in the back door because it was closest to the spot he'd found to park. He'd taken his time making his way through the kitchen because he knew she was here.

She was—looking small and feminine and utterly desirable. She'd leaned forward so she could hear what Amber was saying. The gesture allowed her hair to flow over her shoulder. Tanner tried not to focus on the strands touching the upper mounds of her breasts. Tried and failed.

How many times had he come within a heartbeat of driving over to the clinic, or stopping by her place after work, or picking up the telephone? How many times had he convinced himself she didn't need another argument from him and, even if it killed her in the end, she had a right to time alone with Amber.

He'd told himself he was being noble and unselfish by keeping his distance. Now he knew the truth. He couldn't look at her without remembering the heat and movement, the passion of their time together. The life in that small body.

How could Chris put her through hell?

Was there anything he could do to protect her from any more hell?

"You're staring, man."

Tanner whirled. Just behind him stood Red, a goofy smile on his face. "Don't you know better than to sneak up on an old man," Tanner accused. "You want to give me a heart attack?"

"If you keel over from a bad ticker, it won't be me who gave it to you. The lady isn't bad-looking, is she? Of course I thought that from the beginning, but in that dress . . ."

Tanner knew Red was joking. The younger man was head over heels in lust after one of the hospital admissions clerks. Just the same, he didn't particularly like knowing that Melaine had caught more than one man's eye, or that his fixation on her had been that obvious. He reminded Red that the admissions clerk had said she'd drop by when she got off work.

"In twenty minutes, but who's counting." Red grinned. "Go talk to her, will you? Whatever's gone sour between the two of you isn't worth it."

"What makes you think something's gone sour?"

"Are you kidding?" Red shook his head. "You've been about as much fun to work with lately as the proverbial bear coming out of hibernation. She has that little girl with her again, doesn't she? What's wrong? The kid doesn't like you?"

Tanner wished it was that simple. He managed to extricate himself from Red, but that meant he was now in the living room. He wasn't dense. He guessed that everyone here was aware that he and Melaine had been seeing each other. If he didn't say something to her, there'd be more speculation than he cared to think about.

"Melaine. You're looking nice." He winced. A fourteen-year-old could come up with a better opener than that.

She turned quickly, as if she'd been waiting for him. At least Amber had wandered off. They'd have some privacy, even if he didn't know how to handle it. "Tanner." She didn't smile. Yet he saw, or thought he saw, her features soften. He'd always been aware of her large, expressive eyes. Now, with that faint touch of color highlighting her lids, they seemed enormous.

"You've been busy?" Good. Another piece of brilliant dialogue.

"Busy. Nothing out of the ordinary, though."

"That's good. And Amber? She's been keeping busy?"

"I enrolled her in the local school. I couldn't see her staying out that long. I don't know why Chris didn't think of that." Her mouth, her full and inviting mouth, thinned. "I'm sorry. You don't want to talk about that, do you?"

"That's not it." Everyone had gravitated to Bert and Carol's living room. He touched Melaine's elbow, indicating they might slip into an unoccupied corner. To his relief, she didn't pull away. Still, it would have been a lot easier if she wasn't standing so close. "I don't mind talking about him," he said. "Or Amber. It's just that we don't see things the same way."

"No." She sounded sad. "We don't."

He didn't have to go on touching her. Still, it had been so long. Too long. "I wish it didn't have to be like this."

"Do you mean that?" Melaine asked, her voice quavering a little.

"You have to ask?" As someone bumped her arm, Melaine almost lost her balance. Tanner backed her into a corner and stood sentry. She seemed so tiny to him with that whisper of a dress skimming over her breasts and hugging her waist. The skirt slithered over her hips; he forced his fingers to remain by his side. "Melaine, I'd hoped I wouldn't have to say this. That you'd understand. There's nothing I want more than your happiness."

Melaine blinked. When she opened her eyes, the new sheen caught the lights. "I thought about you," she said. "It's been snowing almost every day. I think about you, and the other patrol members, struggling to stay ahead of things."

"I don't know if I'd call it a struggle," Tanner said, although he couldn't care less about his job. "It's hard thinking of snow as a problem when I have the mountain to myself."

Melaine cocked her head to the side. He sensed a subtle relaxation in her. "To yourself?" she asked. "But what about all the skiers?"

"They stay to the trails, the runs, waiting in line for the lifts. Most of them don't know or care about the rest of the mountain."

"Tell me about it."

For a moment Tanner thought she might just be making conversation, but then he looked, really looked, at her. She wanted to hear about what he experienced when he was away from the crowds. "Dawn is the best time," he began. "Especially if it snowed during the night. Yesterday morning the sun came out for a while. The snow looked as if someone had sprinkled diamonds through it. I skied a little west of where you and I went the day we climbed. There's a little valley tucked between two peaks. It's a bit of a hike getting to it, but once there . . ." Caught in the memory, Tanner let his voice trail off. When he felt Melaine's eyes on him, he continued. "For about three miles, it's the purest form of cross-country skiing there is. I heard a couple of coyotes. Except for that, I was alone."

"Alone."

"Right in the middle of nature. I didn't have a whole lot of time, so I couldn't stay there long, but the run down—they say there isn't much powder at Mammoth. For the most part they're right, but I kicked up a fine spray. I don't know how fast I was going. Fast. But it didn't seem like it. I drifted. That's what it felt like. Skiing the clouds."

Melaine didn't speak. Tanner turned his final words around in his mind. *Skiing the clouds*. He'd never thought of himself as having a poetic soul, but he'd wanted to share something rich and rare with Melaine, and this seemed the way to do it. It had worked. Her eyes glistening with excitement and her mouth open and smiling told him he'd handed her everything he had to offer of his adventure.

"I'd like to take you there," he said, not knowing he was going to say it until the words were out. "At dawn. With the sun turning the snow to diamonds and a coyote singing, and no one but us out there."

"Oh, Tanner. I wish—"

"Don't wish, Melaine. It can happen."

Can it? Oh, he believed it. Listening to him, sharing with him, Melaine believed it, too. Only, they were more than a man and a woman with dreams of floating down a silent mountain together. Her heart belonged to more than just him.

And at the moment, that someone was begging to spend the night with Bert and Carol Edmonds. "Carol says I can help her feed the horses in the morning. I can put on the bells they wear when they pull the sleigh through the town. And I can sit next to Carol when she takes the tourists for a ride. Melaine? Please?"

"Yes, Melaine, please. There's no school tomorrow."

Melaine laughed at Carol's attempt at a whine. "You're ganging up on me," she said, forcing her eyes off Tanner. She had no idea how long they'd talked, only that she'd resented it when a couple of men interrupted them a few minutes ago.

"I admit it." Carol punched Amber playfully on the shoulder. "If I'm going to be a mother, I'd better learn how to talk kid talk. Amber says she remembers what it's like to be a baby. She's agreed to give me some pointers. Besides . . ." Carol winked. "If Amber bunks with me, that leaves you free to do whatever it is you and a certain someone want to."

Melaine was glad Carol hadn't said any more than that. If she had, Amber might have asked another of her questions. Melaine hugged Amber good-bye, watching as Carol and Amber disappeared into the kitchen. For an instant she fought the need to run after the girl and hold her to her. She'd be gone so soon!

But the stark terror that had overwhelmed her the night Chris dropped his bomb had become something almost manageable. She'd weathered so much since Chris and Amber became part of her life. Somehow she'd find a way through this new upheaval.

Besides, Tanner was beside her.

"I heard," he said softly. "Amber won't be with you tonight."

"No. I'm playing second fiddle to a barn full of draft horses."

"It happens to the best of us. I'd like to leave now. And I'd like you to come with me."

"I—brought the Jeep."

"We'll get it in the morning."

Tanner's request was simple and straightforward. All it required was a straightforward answer. Only, with him standing so close that simply by rotating her wrist she could run her nails over his thigh, Melaine had to struggle to remember how to speak. So much still stood between them, might always stand between them. But they'd found a beautiful common ground. She loved hearing about Tanner's early-morning adventures on the mountain. She wanted to tell him about the athletic teenager who'd dropped by the clinic a couple of days ago. The boy had dreams of becoming a doctor and saw his physical prowess as a key to the scholarships that would turn dream into reality. She hadn't told anyone about two hours of charged, nonstop conversation that transcended any generational gaps.

Tanner would understand what it had meant to be able to share her passion for nursing with a bright young man.

But that wasn't the only reason she followed Tanner into a bedroom to search for their coats.

The temperature had dropped below freezing. As a consequence, a glistening, silvered crust now coated roofs, fences, trees, turning Mammoth into a snow-silenced wonderland. Melaine sat next to Tanner as he drove slowly down deserted streets. From inside the many condos and motels, lights shone and an occasional window revealed groups of people gathered around fireplaces. Still, most of the village remained dressed in shadows. Those shadows drew Melaine. She rested her hand on Tanner's knee, thinking of the twists and turns their relationship had taken.

It was incredible. Despite everything that should have torn them apart, they were still together.

"I wish I had a camera that would capture this," Tanner said. He pointed toward a Swedish-style apartment, its cornice studded with frozen snow crystals. "I don't think I'll ever be able to look at what snow can accomplish without being moved by it."

"That's a beautiful sentiment."

"Is it?" Tanner placed his right hand over Melaine's. His left gripped the steering wheel firmly, ready in case the tires failed to find something to hug. "I don't say these things to the men I work with. Maybe they'd understand. Probably. But I have a certain image to project. Macho, for lack of a better word."

Macho was the perfect word to describe Tanner Harris. At least it would be if a person didn't look beneath the surface. But Melaine had. She knew about a man almost undone by the purity of a silent, snow-coated dawn. She'd watched him grapple with the intensity of what she felt for Amber. She'd been able to talk to him about her childhood, knowing he'd respect her confidence.

"Is that hard? Having to project yourself in a certain way to gain the respect and confidence of the patrol members, skiers?"

"Not usually." Tanner ran his fingers over Melaine's knuckle and then began a slow, sensual journey from wrist to forearm. "I think image is written somewhere in the job description. It's become second nature with me. If I sound confident, then those around me tend to act the same."

Melaine brushed her tongue over her upper lip, surrendering to the promise in a touch. "It's the same for a nurse. If she doesn't panic, if she remains professional, no matter what the situation, it helps the patient."

"We can fall apart later."

"Thank heavens. I remember my first car accident after I started working in the emergency room. Three teenagers, thankfully none of them badly wounded. But they'd all been cut and were bleeding pretty badly. One girl lost it. I actually had to slap her to get her to stop screaming."

"After everyone had been stitched up, what did you do?"

Melaine winced, but gave Tanner an honest answer. "I went into the nurses's lounge and broke down. My supervisor found me. I was sure she'd ball me out, but she said it was all right to cry."

"Backlash," Tanner said as he pulled next to his cabin. "We can't protect ourselves against that, can we? It's part of being human."

Melaine waited until Tanner had turned off the engine. "Do you tell your employees it's all right for them to cave in once the emergency is over?"

"Yeah. I do. I worked with an old ranger who maintained that a real man never shows emotion. *He* didn't. He also drank himself to sleep a lot of nights. I decided I'd never try to deny what I felt. Like tonight." Tanner turned toward Melaine, his features nothing more than a deep haze in the unlighted cab. "I want to spend the night with you. I want it to be right for us, and if that means not talking—"

"Not talking?"

"About what we can't do anything about, at least not now."

Blinking back tears, Melaine could only nod and collapse against the strength she'd come to know so well.

Even with everything that stood between them, he wasn't turning his back on her. At least not now. "Tonight," she managed. "That's all we have, isn't it?"

"That's all anyone has. One hour. One night at a time."

When dawn finally touched its fingers to the multitude of ice crystals that bathed Mammoth Lakes, Melaine had learned something precious. It was possible to lose oneself in the night.

She lay in a limbo between sleep and wakefulness, aware of nothing except the warm, naked strength beside her. With fingers that now knew his body as well as they knew her own, she touched a thumb to Tanner's left nipple. They hadn't done much talking, not because there were that many subjects they didn't dare broach, but because the communication they needed and wanted didn't take words.

Melaine drank deeply of Tanner's scent. The echo of aftershave and soap and dried sweat had already become part of her. Yet with this breath, even more of him entered her. He was a wonderful lover—controlled power in strong, silken hands. They'd danced together. The dance had been played out to the tune of nothing more than the music inside her.

Reluctant to let go of the night and yet knowing she needed to return to the real world, Melaine opened her eyes. Despite the cool room, Tanner slept with one arm outside the blankets. She focused on that. Even in sleep, the image of strength remained. As a nurse she could name the different muscles, tendons, bones, but this morning she felt nothing like a nurse.

She thought of hard cords of power beneath work-tempered flesh. His arm had held her safe and strong against him as they made love. If she asked, would that same arm remain there for her for the rest of her life . . . ?

The thought washed away what remained of the night.

She hadn't considered that before, hadn't let herself. But the hours of exploration and lovemaking made the question necessary. Like her, Tanner wasn't someone who easily gave himself to another. He turned feminine heads. She never doubted that. But if there'd been many women in his life, she would have known. He'd have treated her casually, quickly, sliding over foreplay so he could satisfy his own physical needs. He hadn't done that. Instead he'd asked with words and gestures what she needed out of their time together. What he could give her.

Tomorrow. She wanted him to give her tomorrow.
She didn't know how to ask.

"You're awake."

At Tanner's words, Melaine started. She hadn't had enough time alone with her thoughts. "It—looks that way. What about you?"

"I'm thinking about it," he said and captured her against him. Flesh met flesh and Melaine wondered if they might never get out of bed.

"Thinking about it? Is that possible?" she asked.

"Oh, yes," he told her wisely. "I've made a decision." He ran his tongue over her ear, chuckling and holding on when she tried to squirm free.

"A decision?"

"Serious one. World-shattering serious."

"What?"

"It's going to call for a major decision on your part."

"Oh."

"As much as I'd like to spend the day chewing on your ear, I have something on my mind." He pushed her a few inches away and cupped her breast beneath the blanket. "A decision we have to make."

Melaine tensed. "A decision?" she managed. Was he going to end this escape from reality so easily?

"Yep. What's for breakfast? I'm starving."

Starving? Melaine took a deep breath, relaxing. Now that she thought about it, her stomach felt hollowed out.

She'd had more than enough to eat last night, but hours of lovemaking burned up an incredible number of calories. "All this was so you could tell me you were hungry?" Melaine pretended indignation but doubted she'd fooled him. "And I suppose you're going to tell me you want me to do something about it."

"It crossed my mind."

Over toast and eggs, Tanner explained that he'd be spending the day back on June Mountain. "I wish I didn't have to leave. I feel so far from you over there. But you'll have Amber."

Melaine nodded.

Tanner placed a forkful of scrambled eggs on his toast and chewed. He picked up his coffee, then set it back down again. Melaine felt the change in him even before he spoke. "Do you know what Chris and I talked about?" he asked. "I asked him why he wouldn't give you custody. He said something about his parents and responsibility."

Chilled, Melaine wrapped her hands around her mug. "It'd make sense if you knew his folks."

"Tell me about them."

This wasn't how she wanted their time together to end, but Melaine didn't sidestep Tanner's request. "I never saw that much of them. Whenever they came to visit, they spent most of their time talking about Chris's business or Amber's progress. It was as if she was some kind of acquisition. I don't know if I ever saw them simply hug her. Amber didn't get excited when we told her her grandparents were coming. She should have, you know."

"Why didn't she?"

Her appetite forgotten, Melaine tried to concentrate. "I believe children have an instinct about the adults they come in contact with. They might not be able to articulate things, but they know. Chris's parents aren't demonstrative people."

"Cold."

"Yes," Melaine agreed. "Cold. Contained. I've never seen a woman as contained as Chris's mother. His father could get excited about a business deal, especially if he was able to show his superiority over an adversary. He and Chris would talk for hours about competition and effective advertising and a dozen other things that quite frankly bored me. But I often wondered what they'd talk about if they didn't have that."

"Did you and your mother-in-law have much in common?"

"Almost nothing. She's one of the best golfers I've ever seen. She has trophies, awards. But then she has the time and means to play the game as much as she wants to." Melaine rested her elbows on the table. She tried to picture Margaret Landa carrying on a conversation with Tanner but couldn't think of a single common thread. "I don't mean to make it sound as if she doesn't do anything important with her life. She's involved in local politics. She's an incredibly successful fund-raiser, and she has spearheaded several successful campaigns. But politics isn't a passion of mine. I wanted to talk to Margaret about Amber."

"Then what you're saying is that Chris inherited his contained nature. His parents weren't demonstrative toward him when he was a child and that's the way he approaches parenthood."

"Yes," Melaine said softly. No matter how much Chris frustrated her, she could feel sorry for him. "Amber's not like that, thank heavens. She leads with her heart. From what I've heard, her mother was warm and outgoing. Did you know—no, of course you don't. Margaret said that when Chris's first wife died, he didn't cry. *I* never saw him cry."

"No. He wouldn't."

Tanner's insight into Chris's makeup caught Melaine a little off guard. But something must have happened while the two men were together that had taught Tanner a great deal about Chris. "That's why I have to be part of Amber's life. She needs to feel free to laugh and cry."

"You never could convince Chris of that, could you?"

Melaine shook her head. She felt as if she'd been plucked, struggling, out of the world she'd lost herself in last night and dropped back into one without doors or windows. Once again she was trapped. "His parents failed him in a lot of ways. But they did instill in him a deep sense of responsibility. That's what Amber is to him. An obligation. He's a single parent, not because—not because he truly loves her—although I think he does as much as he's capable, but because he has to live up to his parents' expectations."

For a long time Tanner said nothing. He toyed with his breakfast but didn't eat. Melaine stood in one corner of her cage, wondering if, by some miracle, he might be able to reach through the bars and find a way to free her.

"Accept it," he said finally. His words echoed in the too-quiet room. "You can't change Chris. You have to accept it."

"I can't."

"You don't have a choice, Melaine. Damn, we've been over this before. I don't want to come back to it any more than you do, but I guess it has to be said. Do what you can for Amber. Remain a positive influence in her life. Spend your vacations in Aspen if that's what you want to do. Have her spend part of her summers with you. But don't turn your back on a life of your own because of her."

Melaine's head throbbed. She couldn't bear to look at Tanner. "You don't know what you're asking."

"Don't I? I think I'm the only one who's looking at this realistically. What you're doing now isn't good for her. It's giving her mixed signals, keeping her off balance. And it sure as hell isn't good for you."

"You don't love her." Melaine spoke around the hard

and painful thudding of her heart. "That's the difference between you and me. You don't love her."

Tanner stood. Silent, he carried his plate to the sink and then turned around. He looked down at her, his eyes a hundred years older than they'd been when he woke up this morning. "No. I don't. I haven't allowed that to happen."

"Allow?" In her pain, Melaine spat out the word. "That's how you see it? Allow? Tanner, love isn't like that."

"Isn't it? We're intelligent, reasoning human beings, Melaine. As such, we have control over our lives, our emotions."

"Maybe you do," Melaine managed as she got to her feet. "If that's how it is, then I feel sorry for you."

"Sorry?"

"For—" She stared at him, feeling too much, wishing she could go cold and dead inside. "I might hurt. I might feel pain. But at least I've experienced every emotion life has to offer. You said you and your wife drifted apart. Are you sure that's it? Maybe you didn't have enough to give her."

"You believe that?"

"I don't know what goes on inside you." Every word she spoke brought pain; yet she couldn't stop herself. "But if you think love is an emotion you can turn on or off, or put up barriers against . . . Never mind." Melaine turned toward the door. "We don't even speak the same language, do we?"

THIRTEEN

After a valiant struggle, Melaine managed to smile. "It's all set," she told Amber the day after returning from Tanner's. "You and I are going skiing."

"All right! We don't have to go too fast, do we?"

Remembering Amber's experience when she and her father went cross-country together, Melaine assured the girl that they had all day. She'd gotten Red to cover for her at the clinic, and as soon as they were ready, she and Amber would head to Lakes Basin and the groomed cross-country trails there. She knew enough to inform the ski patrol of her plans, but she hadn't told Tanner.

She wasn't going to.

Fortunately, Amber was too excited to notice her silence. Amber chatted while Melaine prepared breakfast and threw together something for lunch. She was still talking when Melaine herded her into the bedroom to dress. Melaine stepped into her own room and reached for her ski outfit. She slipped out of her robe and reached for a turtleneck sweater. For a moment weakness almost overtook her, but she fought it off.

She'd put a necessary end to a bad marriage. If she and Tanner couldn't resolve their differences . . .

No. She wouldn't think about that. Today was for

Amber and fresh air and, maybe, clearing her head and heart.

The weather forecast was for a cloudy morning giving way to a clear afternoon. Although Melaine figured Amber would have enough skiing after about three hours, she was glad to hear they wouldn't have to contend with snow should their outing turn out to take longer than that. She loaded skis, poles, and backpacks into her Jeep, and with Amber still chattering beside her, took off. Melaine kept up her end of the conversation, but that didn't stop her thoughts. In nine days, she would have to pack Amber's belongings.

There were three other cars parked at the side of the road that led to Lakes Basin, but she couldn't see anything of the other skiers. After making sure their bindings were secure, Melaine took off on the well-groomed trail with Amber close behind. Amber was a little disgruntled because Melaine's camera was awkward for her to operate, but before they'd gone a quarter of a mile, she regained her sense of humor.

"I bet there's a lot of gold here. I asked Carol and she said maybe I was right. Do you think we could get a mine and—what is it we would have to do?"

Melaine wasn't sure. She shared what little she knew of mining techniques, aware that today she was building a memory. She had no idea when she'd see Amber again. Pictures and snatches of conversation might be all she had to get her through the winter—especially if she and Tanner couldn't make their peace with each other.

"Melaine?"

"What, honey?"

"Why isn't Tanner with us?"

"Tanner?" Melaine stumbled over the word. "He has to work. Not everyone gets to play hookey like you and me."

"Oh. Are you going to marry him?"

"What?" Melaine glanced back at Amber. "What made you ask that?"

"Daddy said. When he told me about moving and I cried, he said I shouldn't be sad for you because you and Tanner might get married. He said . . . he said you wouldn't have time for me anymore."

Although it was difficult for them to make any progress if they skied side by side, Melaine pulled back until she kept pace with Amber. Speaking around the solid lump in her throat, she said, "There's no such thing as not having time for you, honey. I fell in love with you the first day I saw you, and that's never changed. Even when you dressed up like a witch for Halloween, I still loved you."

"Not a witch. I was a mad scientist."

"That's right." Melaine smiled, grateful for Amber's ability to switch easily from a somber topic to one with humor in it. "A mad scientist who dressed in black and wore huge hats to hide his chemicals in. About what your father said. He's wrong. It doesn't matter what happens to either of us, I'll always find time for you."

"Even if you and Tanner have a baby of your own?"

"A baby? Honey, Tanner and I aren't married."

"But when you do, you're going to want a baby, aren't you?"

When? If only life was as simple as Amber wanted it to be. "I don't know what's going to happen. Tanner and I haven't said anything about getting married. We have some problems—a big one. If that can't be worked out, then neither of us is going to want to get married."

Amber seemed to be thinking that over. Melaine tried to concentrate on skiing, but it was all but impossible. No matter where she looked, she could picture Tanner here. He'd love this easy, isolated trail. He'd keep his eyes on the sky, hoping for a glimpse of an eagle above the treetops. From what Melaine knew of the trail, soon they'd be much closer to the mountains. Steep, snow-covered peaks would block out much of the sun, but that wouldn't bother Tanner. He'd turn his attention to the snow masses, mentally judging their stability and deciding when and if some of the load needed to be lessened. If he was here, maybe he'd tell her that nothing stood between them and a peaceful, memory-filled outing.

Only, he wasn't here. He hadn't asked about her plans for the day, and she hadn't told him.

"Do you love Tanner?"

Melaine wasn't ready for Amber's question. Pretending she needed to reposition her backpack, she stalled. Love? What did a woman who hadn't received enough of it from her parents, who had chosen a distant and contained man to marry, know about the emotion? Finally, though, there was no avoiding Amber's question. "Love isn't as simple as they try to make it sound in the stories I've read to you," she admitted. "In fact, the older you get, the more complicated love becomes."

"It wasn't for Cinderella and Prince Charming. They lived happily ever after."

No they hadn't. At least that had been the conclusion she and Tanner had come to. "I wonder. Maybe Cinderella wasn't a good cook and the prince got mad when she burned things."

"Oh. Do you think?"

"I don't know, honey. But Cinderella was make-believe. Everything's harder in the real world."

"Is love too—complicated for you and Tanner?"

Melaine wondered if she'd ever tell Tanner what Amber just said. Maybe; if she did, he'd understand how special the girl was. And maybe it was too late for them to talk. About Amber. And about a simple word neither she nor Tanner had spoken. "I don't know. Sometimes I think so."

"Because of me?"

Melaine jammed her poles into the ground, stopping her forward motion. Blinking back tears, she turned toward Amber. "No. Not because of you. You're the best thing that's ever happened to me. Tanner knows that. He likes you." Melaine avoided the word love. "But you're a very intelligent young lady. You know how complicated things are for us because of the way your daddy and you live, the way I live. Having Tanner around, well, that just makes it all the more complicated."

Amber sighed. "I wish it was different," she said softly. "I wish I lived with you."

"I—I wish you did, too."

"I could visit Daddy just the way I visit you now. I could live here and go to school here and Bert could fly me to Aspen whenever Daddy had time." Amber's features clouded. "Do you think Tanner would like that?"

"Tanner? I don't know." Melaine drank deeply of snow-scented air, desperate to clear away the tears that seemed to fill her.

"You could ask him."

If only it was that simple. If only they had some bond, like whispered words of love. Because of their skis, it was impossible for Melaine to reach out for a hug. Instead she smiled and winked at Amber. "You're pretty serious, you know that. Today we're supposed to be having an adventure."

Because she had no goal in mind, Melaine didn't care when, a little after 11 A.M., Amber declared she was starving. They stopped near a rocky outcropping for sandwiches, cheese, and apple juice. They spent several minutes taking pictures of each other. Then, when Amber was ready, they headed back into the wilderness. Melaine had told Amber to let her know when she wanted to turn around, but Amber wanted to see if she could go farther and longer than she and her father had. As long as they didn't go too fast, she wasn't the least bit tired.

Melaine let Amber lead the way for the next half mile, but when the valley narrowed down and the peaks pressed in, she skied around the girl. Amber had a tendency to forget where she was going while she talked and stared at the scenery. If there were any spots the grooming equipment had missed, Melaine would be able to point them out. A couple of times she thought she heard other voices, but because the wind was blowing and their skis made a constant whooshing sound, she couldn't be sure. She hoped they wouldn't come across any other groups, that she wouldn't have to share Amber with anyone.

"Do they have girl rangers?" Amber asked on the tail end of a five-minute-long monologue about math versus reading classes and how much she liked working a calculator. "That's what I want to be when I grow up."

"I know they do. We have a couple working here. What do you think you'd like the most about being a ranger?"

"Telling people what they can and can't do." Amber laughed. "Not really. Daddy has to be indoors so much. I hate it. It's funny. Daddy sells skis and he hardly ever gets to go skiing. Do you think I really could get good enough to be in the Olympics?"

"They don't let chatterboxes in the Olympics." Curious as to how Amber would respond to that, Melaine started to turn around. For a moment she thought she'd run into a bunch of rocks. She reached out, trying to regain her balance. Amber, too, had begun to shake as if pulled by invisible strings. The world around them joined in the powerful, insane tremor.

Amber screamed. Melaine reached for her. Then, with a roar like a train from hell, the crag above them shuddered and threw off its mantle of snow. Yelling, Melaine dove for Amber, shoving her out of the way.

"Everyone! Out! You all know the drill. Get on your walkie-talkies. We need damage reports. Cliff, make damn sure the lifts shut down!"

Tanner whirled from the speaker system that connected him to every member of the ski patrol, his hand snaking out to grab his skis. A moment before, he'd been sitting inside the base ski patrol office trying to concentrate on paperwork. Then the chair he'd been sitting in slid halfway across the floor with him in it, and he knew his worst fears had been realized.

Mammoth Lakes had been hit by an earthquake.

He could have waited for preliminary information about the magnitude about the quake, but that didn't matter. The slopes were filled with skiers, and unless a miracle had happened, some of them would be injured. His greatest concern wasn't so much for those in the well-designed lifts but for anyone who might have been in the way of an avalanche.

Throwing his skis over his shoulder, Tanner sprinted for his truck. He could be reached via his C.B. In the meantime, he intended to get as close to the areas of congestion as possible. As he drove, tires squealing, he prayed. An aftershock forced him to steer back onto the right side of the road. Despite the adrenaline coursing through him, he slowed. It wouldn't do to have the director injured.

His mind ticked through the necessary steps. As he'd drilled into his co-workers, it was essential that they have an overall picture of the situation. The hospital and first-aid stations would be setting up to accept the wounded, but first those casualties had to be brought in for treatment. That was his job, his responsibility.

He felt exhausted. At the same time, he felt as if he could run on pure nerve for the next week.

An hour later all of his rangers had reported in. He'd also had contact with each lift. Preliminary reports made him hopeful that no one had been killed. One lift had become disabled with about twenty people trapped in their chairs. Fortunately, no one had been injured, but it would be a while before they could be freed. Tanner left that task up to the lift operators and volunteer rescuers.

He pulled in at Mid-Chalet. From what he'd been told, a number of skiers in the area had been in the way of an avalanche and rescue operations were in full force. Leaving his truck running, Tanner sprinted toward the run. The quick-thinking lift operator had unloaded his passengers and told them all to go home. The lift was now free to carry patients down to the waiting four-wheel drive vehicles that served as ambulances. Tanner pulled his walkie-talkie from his belt, thinking to let Melaine know she'd soon have injured skiers heading her way. Instead he found himself talking to an agitated Red.

"She isn't here, Chief. I thought you knew. She took the day off to be with that little girl. I've got a doctor who just walked in the door and offered to help, so we'll be all right."

"The day off? Where is she?"

"She said something about their going cross-country skiing."

What had been raw energy became dread. So far only a handful of cross-country skiers had returned. The rest were out there, isolated. Maybe in trouble.

At least she had the good sense to report in, Tanner thought when he learned that she and Amber had gone to Lakes Basin. Bert Edmonds was already flying over the area. His in-the-air report chilled Tanner's blood. "It's not pretty," he said over the static. "Four, five slides. I've had a couple of groups wave at me. None of them look frantic, but that doesn't account for everyone who headed out there this morning. I'm going to get a little closer, but we're going to need ground rescue."

Tanner had already sent a group of trained volunteers to Lakes Basin. Now, when he contacted them, he couldn't keep the tension out of his voice. "I'm going to join you," he told the leader. "Things look fairly under control on the slopes. It's the remote areas I'm worried about."

After being told that the leader agreed, Tanner turned

off the walkie-talkie. Everything in him screamed for action, but there was one more thing he wanted to do before jumping back in his truck. He didn't know how to contact Chris, but he had the name of the man's factory in Bishop. The receptionist gave him the number of Chris's hotel in Aspen. Finally, Tanner got Chris on the line.

"I wanted you to know," he said, not bothering with more than the briefest introduction, "we've had an earthquake out here. Melaine and Amber are among the missing."

"What? Has anyone been killed?"

"Not that we know of. Look, I've got to—"

"I know. You've got the manpower for that kind of operation?"

"Yeah," Tanner said. "We'll find her. We've already got a rescue crew in that area. I'll be joining them in a few minutes. I just hope . . ." He stopped, unable to make himself say he hoped Amber and Melaine were still alive. "Damn. There's just no way we could have predicted this."

"I know that. Look, ah . . . Never mind. I won't keep you."

Two vehicles in addition to those used by the volunteers were parked at the side of the road when Tanner arrived. One of them was Melaine's Jeep. The volunteers had rounded up a number of snowmobiles and were already on their way. Grabbing the one that had been left for him, Tanner took off at a speed he'd never sanction. As he drove, he remained in touch with base operations. The first casualties were now being treated. Those hung up in the lift should be safely on the ground in a few more minutes. Two buildings in old Mammoth had collapsed, but the newer structures had survived the quake with only broken windows. Most gratifying of all, everyone on the slopes had been accounted for, in one way or another.

That left the cross-country ski trails—one of them the trail Melaine had taken.

Three miles from the road, Tanner caught up with the rest of the snowmobilers. They'd been stopped by a massive slide, and the volunteers were in the process of strapping on their skis.

"It's kinda funny," the middle-aged leader said when Tanner joined him. "I always thought a rescue operation would be an adventure. The kind of thing to tell my grandkids. But the truth? Right now I'm scared to death we're going to find something I don't want to."

Tanner swallowed and felt blood. He'd bit the inside of his mouth without knowing it. "We don't have a choice," he managed. "We have to go out there."

The man glanced skyward. "We're not going to have much time. We have about two hours of daylight left."

Two hours. Was it enough? Or maybe Melaine was past caring about time. Because standing still made him feel as if he was falling apart, Tanner sprinted back to his snowmobile and jammed on his skis. He grabbed his walkie-talkie, a flashlight, the lightweight rescue sled. Then, his heart hammering, he led the way.

It took the better part of an hour to claw their way over the avalanche. Because the cross-country trails braided through Lakes Basin, Tanner dispatched the volunteers in all directions with instructions that they keep in constant contact with him. Knowing the others could reach him in a matter of minutes, he elected to travel alone.

Hell couldn't be any worse than this, Tanner thought as the sun plowed its way toward the horizon. He'd felt heartened when one of the teams came across the other missing skiers—a young couple. The woman was pregnant and they'd wisely decided to travel slowly. No. They hadn't seen anything of a woman and a girl. Yes. There'd been a number of avalanches around the crags.

It was the silence. If he had someone to talk to, he wouldn't have to listen to his brain crashing against one nightmare possibility after another. Melaine and Amber had been crushed beneath tons of snow. It'd be weeks before their bodies were located. No! He couldn't face that possibility. They'd been trapped and had no choice but to wait until someone arrived to dig them out. But help couldn't find them before nightfall, and they'd have to wait in the dark, injured, until morning.

Maybe time would run out for them then.

Tanner slowed and bent over, clamping his hand over the nausea churning inside. No! He couldn't think about that, either.

But what choice did he have? If they were all right, they would have found their way out by now. If a pregnant woman could make it . . .

Don't think, Tanner warned himself. He glanced down at the walkie-talkie clamped to his waist, begging the instrument to come to life with the news he needed to hear. *Look. Listen. Keep moving. Pray. Only, don't think thoughts that'll drive you insane.*

Tanner's thighs ached and his left foot felt pinched because he hadn't taken time to position his sock properly. His throat ached from calling Melaine and Amber's names. He'd lived with a headache so long that he'd forgotten there was any other way to feel. At least the headache kept other thoughts from taking over everything.

A sound? No. It had to be the ramblings of a madman. Still, Tanner paused, trying to isolate something different from the sound of the wind in the trees. He felt as if he'd been swallowed by snow and had to struggle against a terrifying sense of claustrophobia he never thought he'd experience.

Wait! Tanner had been about to start skiing again when the sound that had caught his attention was repeated.

FOURTEEN

The child in the red-and-white outfit sank to her hips in the snow, but before Tanner could reach her, she pulled herself free and began scrambling forward on hands and knees again. Despite the almost overwhelming need to take Amber in his arms, Tanner literally couldn't move. Relief exploded through him, nearly bringing him to his knees. It had been four hours since the earthquake hit. He had a pretty good idea what that time had been like for the girl. Damn it! He would have done anything to spare her.

"Amber! It's me. Tanner."

At this call, Amber rocked back on her haunches and lifted her head. A shaky smile, punctuated by tears, transformed the grim set to her features. "Tanner? Really?"

"Really. You look wonderful. Do you have any idea how wonderful you look?"

"I can't walk. Every time I stand up, I sink down, deep. I'm *so* tired."

"I know." Quickly Tanner skied to her side. He reached out to assist her, but when she came off her knees, he did more than guide her to packed snow. Despite her long arms and legs, she fit in his arms. She weighed enough that he had to brace himself in order to hold her, but he needed the contact. The proof that the suddenly unbelievably precious child really was alive.

"You're squeezing me."

Tanner didn't care. Hours of tension poured out of him. He clutched Amber to him, his cheek pressed tightly against hers. He took a deep breath and then another, trying to still the erratic beating of his heart. He felt her hot, wet tears—or were they his? He'd expected to feel this relief when and if he found Melaine, but to experience such emotion around a child he barely knew . . .

"Tanner. You're squeezing me."

"I know." Slowly, reluctantly, he set her down, careful to find a spot that would support her weight. He dropped to his knees in front of her and cupped his gloves around her frozen, bare fingers. "That's what people do when they're happy to see someone else."

"I know. Melaine and I do that every time. Tanner? What's wrong?"

Tanner blinked. Something hot burned against his lids, and he blinked again. "What do you mean?"

"You're crying. How come you're crying?"

She was right. Tanner tried smiling; now something lodged in his throat. He felt weak with gratitude that the mountain hadn't claimed this young life. He didn't care if she saw his tears, didn't care that she now knew he was more than a strong, resourceful snow ranger. "I guess . . ." He blew his warm breath over her fingers. "That's another something people do when they're very glad to see someone. You're all right? You're really all right?"

"I'm hungry. Really hungry. I'm tired of falling down. I lost my gloves. Melaine gave them to me, and I lost them. We have to get back. Tanner? Melaine needs help."

Melaine. "What do you mean, help?"

"She hurt herself. She pushed me aside when the avalanche came, and almost got buried."

"Buried?" Tanner tasted the bitter, frightening word. "You . . . How was she when you last saw her?"

"Her side hurt. Bad." Amber's lips trembled. "She tried not to let it show, but I knew. She couldn't stand. She showed me where she wanted me to walk." Amber pointed toward a snow-blunted peak. "She said if I walked straight and kept to my right, I would find the road. I was scared. I didn't want to leave her."

"You did right," Tanner said, positioning Amber on the rescue sled. He rubbed her hands vigorously until pale purple was replaced by healthy pink and then handed her a granola bar. "I'm very proud of you. Now, do you think you can show me where you left her?"

Amber hoped so, although with the sun setting, she was afraid she might get confused. Tanner did his best to project a positive image—they'd find Melaine and put her on the sled and get her to the hospital as soon as possible—but with every passing minute, he had to fight his fear. He contacted the other rescuers to let them know he'd found Amber and gave them general directions on where to look for Melaine. He talked to Bert about the possibility of landing near the avalanche site, but Bert was reluctant to attempt that after dark. The best Bert could do was bring the helicopter to a flat valley not quite two miles from where Tanner thought they'd find Melaine.

Hurry. Don't think. Just hurry. Despite her hunger, Amber was in a talkative mood. Tanner sensed that her chatter was a cover-up for her tension, but he welcomed conversation. The energy-filled voice buoyed him. Surrounded by an aura of young life, he was able to keep his own gut-wrenching worry under control. As he skied, dragging Amber behind him, he asked her about her life in Bishop. He was surprised to learn that she had opinions on everything from what car she wanted when she got her driver's license to an appropriate fate for boys who thought it was funny to grab her lunch. Amber was going to be a nurse when she grew up, just like Melaine. It might take her a while to get through college, though, because she was determined to compete in the Olympics. "I want to downhill race. They go *so* fast. You have to be really careful that you don't hit the poles, and you have to wear goggles in case it's snowing. How do they keep their goggles from fogging over? Mine always do."

Tanner didn't have an answer to that, but he did have some suggestions on exercises to strengthen her legs. He didn't point out that the odds of her making the Olympic team were less than the odds of finding Melaine before dark. A child needed dreams and goals. If a dream was squashed instead of encouraged, what would that do to the child's ego?

The sun had set by the time Amber told him the landscape looked like the place they'd been when the accident happened. "Do you think she's really going to be all right?" she asked for the tenth time, her tone fearful. "She said you'd find her, that that's your job. But it's been a long time."

"I know it has." When she first asked, Tanner had thought about trying to downplay Amber's concerns, but he couldn't do that. Just as she needed her dreams, she also needed to understand that the adults in her world weren't miracle workers. "All we can do is try, honey. We won't give up."

"That's what she said. That you wouldn't give up."

For the second time today, Tanner felt the heat of tears. He would have preferred to hunt for Melaine alone because he'd be able to travel twice as fast, but if he had to be held back by anyone, he wanted it to be Amber. "You're a brave young lady," he said, meaning it. "A lot of girls would be afraid to go off by themselves."

"I know," Amber said matter-of-factly. "But I don't get scared much. Did you know Melaine had to take care of her two little sisters when she was growing up. She said people can do anything they put their mind to. When I was getting ready to leave and she couldn't come, she said for me to keep saying, 'I can do it.' "

"She's a very wise woman. And she's right. If we believe we can do something, it makes all the difference."

"I know. Besides, she can't walk. She's depending on me."

And on me, Tanner thought. When Amber started to say something, he held his fingers up to his lips, silencing her. He stopped to still the sound of skis and sled. The wind toying with the evergreens had quieted. "Melaine," he called. "Melaine!"

"Maybe she's too tired to call," Amber whispered after his voice trailed away.

"I'm sure she's tired. But we want her to know we're looking for her." Tanner said nothing about the possibility that Melaine might be in no condition to speak. Instead he bent forward, pulling Amber behind him. Five minutes later he stopped again.

"Melaine! Melaine!"

No answer.

"Tanner?" Amber's tone had turned into that of a child, a young, tired, hungry, scared child. "Do you think maybe we're going the wrong direction?"

"No, honey. I've been following your tracks."

"You have? I fell down a lot. It probably looks like a lot of plops in the snow, doesn't it?"

Tanner swiveled and smiled at Amber. "I'd fall down a lot, too, if I didn't have any skis." He leaned forward and took off again, the dying glow of sunset pressing in around him. Soon he wouldn't be able to see. And Melaine would feel even more alone than she did now—if she was able to feel *any* emotion.

This time he traveled for no more than three minutes before stopping and calling. His voice echoed against the mountain. Then, before silence completely enveloped him, he heard it. A human voice, faint.

"That's her!" Amber shrieked. "I know it!"

"I don't know, honey," Tanner cautioned. "It might

be one of the other searchers. Melaine! Melaine! Can you hear me?"

"Tanner?"

His knees went weak. Stumbling a little in an attempt to regain his balance, Tanner turned back toward Amber. Despite the deep shadows, the girl's face was a study in sunlight. "Melaine," he repeated. "Talk to me. I can't see you."

"Tanner? Oh, God. Amber? Where's Amber?"

Tanner's skiis bit into the snow. He heard Amber grunt as the sled jerked. Instinct as much as his hearing guided him. Melaine was off to his left; he felt her presence. "She's with me," he called out, aware of the difference between his strong voice and Melaine's. Hers quavered with exhaustion and pain. "We're coming. We're coming."

He found her stretched on her side on top of a rubble of snow. Her hair hung limp and wet along her cheeks, giving him little to look at except her eyes. But that was enough; her eyes told him everything.

She'd been through hell today; the taste and smell of it clung to her. Still, her determination held hell at bay. She blinked and focused on him and then Amber. The fear she'd carried in those dark depths evaporated into mist. He would have to wait to learn whether any of that had been for him, or if all her anxiety had been for Amber.

Slipping away from the tow rope, Tanner scrambled over the rough snow. She held out her hand; he reached for it and clutched it to his chest. Then, although she wore gloves, he lifted her hand to his mouth and ran his lips over it. "Thank God," he whispered, his voice strangled. "Thank God."

"Tanner. Amber. Alive."

"Yes, alive. She's been such a trooper. You'll be proud of her. You—how are you?"

Melaine waved away his question. She turned her hand around and laced her fingers through his. He stared down at her, moved by the liquid wash of tears transforming her features. "Cry," he whispered in incredible wisdom. He tried to speak and nearly strangled on the lump in his throat. He swallowed, feeling as if the weight of an entire mountain had just been lifted from him. *Safe. She was safe!* "God knows I've done enough of it today."

"You cried?" Melaine whispered hoarsely as Amber joined them.

"Twice," Amber supplied. "When he found me, and then when we talked about how hard it was to find you." Her voice quavered. "I was so scared, Melaine. I knew I wasn't going to get to the road before dark. But then Tanner found me, and I knew everything would be all right."

"Everything?" Melaine reached for Amber, her eyes still locked on Tanner. "Everything?" She winced when the girl wrapped her arms around her but didn't let go.

Hating the doubt in her voice, the question in her eyes, and yet knowing it had to be, Tanner reached for his walkie-talkie with less than steady fingers. "We'll get you out of here. I promise it."

It was dark by the time the rest of the searchers found Tanner, Melaine, and Amber. After determining that her injuries were confined to her ribs, they gently moved Melaine onto another sled. Tanner pulled her as the group, aided by flashlights, headed toward the meadow where Bert and the helicopter would be waiting.

Melaine, despite the effort of talking, wanted to know everything about the effects of the earthquake. She was grateful to everyone for finding her and getting her out before the temperature dropped below freezing. Again and again, she told Tanner how she'd prayed that he'd find Amber. When one of the rescuers asked what it had been like to spend all that time alone, she hadn't known how to answer. Her mind had been on Amber, not herself.

And Tanner.

There was room for three passengers in the helicopter.

She, Amber, and Tanner went first. Amber did most of the talking during the short flight to the hospital. Tanner sat, cramped, at the foot of the stretcher. Occasionally she lifted her head to look at him, but the raw communication they'd shared on the slope was gone. She couldn't read his thoughts.

She'd broken three ribs.

"I want to go home," she said when finally the doctors were done with her. "There's no reason why I should stay overnight."

Tanner, who'd refused to leave her side while the examination took place, shook his head. "You'd rest better here. You can go home in the morning."

"No I won't. All I want is to get home. I need to have my things around me, to sleep in my own bed."

"You can't climb the stairs."

"All right." Melaine sighed. "So I'll sleep on the couch. Please. Amber needs to get to bed, and I want her with me. I just can't bear the idea of being separated from her again."

Amber was in the hospital cafeteria having dinner with Carol. Melaine hadn't wanted her to go; after the seemingly endless and lonely waiting, the sight of Amber was precious beyond belief. But the girl was starving. Besides, something lay thick and dark around Tanner. No matter what he was thinking, she needed to hear him out—without Amber listening. Melaine cleared her throat. "If you won't do it, I'll ask Carol to drive me."

"She'll have to."

Melaine propped herself up on her elbow, ignoring the wrench in her side. Tanner stood near the window, just far enough away that she couldn't reach out and touch him. "Why? Don't you want to have anything to do with me?"

"That's not it. Melaine, I have to get back to work."

Work? It was now almost 9 p.m. "Why? If you're trying to avoid—"

"I'm not avoiding anything. Look, when I heard you were missing, nothing else mattered. But I've got to get back in touch with my staff, make sure everyone has been accounted for."

Why hadn't she thought of that? "Nothing else mattered?" she managed. The nightmare was behind her. She'd been rescued. More importantly, Amber was safe. Nothing had happened to Tanner. Why then did she still have to constantly battle tears?

"I didn't know where you were." He stepped closer, touching her for the first time since she entered the hospital. "I'm sorry I suggested you stay in the hospital. Of course you'd rather be home near Amber. I just don't like the idea of you not having help around."

"Tanner? I'm all right. Honest."

He lifted her hand toward his mouth again, stopping just short of brushing his lips over her flesh. "I can see that. But I'm having a hard time convincing my heart."

"Your heart?"

Tanner slid his lids down over his eyes. When he opened them again, they remained shuttered as if there was something he wanted or needed to keep from her. "Heart. Head. Everything we've been through—now isn't the time to try to sort it out."

Melaine didn't speak; she couldn't. She drew her hand free, not because she didn't need his warmth on the back of her hand. But he was right. So much had happened between them. Out on the trail, she'd been in too much pain and too relieved to see both him and Amber to do more than send up a prayer of thankfulness. Now she needed to feel his stubbled cheek beneath her fingers, to cup his chin in her palm.

But she couldn't reach him. Not in the only way that counted.

* * *

Amber was asleep by the time Carol carried her up to her room. Carol offered to help Melaine navigate the stairs, but she declined. Despite her physical exhaustion, she was too keyed up to sleep. If Carol would get her a bite to eat and a blanket, she'd spend the night on the couch, she told her friend.

As she nibbled on a sandwich, the two women talked about the damage caused by the earthquake and how wonderful it was that no one had been killed or even badly injured. Melaine was concerned that skiers might stay away from Mammoth, but Carol didn't think so. Skiers were a devoted lot and Californians had learned to accept earthquakes as a fact of life. Melaine asked Carol to thank Bert for her. Any man who could do what he had with a helicopter deserved a medal. Carol thought that if anyone deserved a medal, it was Tanner. His training of the emergency staff had certainly paid off today. "That's what it all boils down to, isn't it? Keeping one's head," Carol said as she got ready to leave. "Talk about a true professional. He's a good man, Melaine. You're lucky to have found him."

Had she? Melaine asked herself once silence overtook the house. She had no doubt that he cared about her. But so much remained unsettled between them—things that even an avalanche couldn't bury.

It was almost 6 A.M. when she heard Tanner's pickup in the drive. She supposed she'd dozed a little, but it had been nothing except naps cut short by nightmares. In her dreams, Amber was the one trapped under tons of snow. Tanner was in a lift; when the earthquake struck, the cable snapped, sending him crashing down to rocks below.

Despite what had to be said, and what might never be said between them, she was grateful to have Tanner put an end to her dreams.

He looked like a man who hadn't slept in weeks. The stubble that had hazed his features in the hospital now gave him an almost hostile look. Because she'd left her door unlocked, he didn't have to wait for her to let him in. He entered without speaking and stood looking down at her.

Say something. Say we'll find a way.

"Sit down. Please," Melaine said when Tanner started to lean against the wall. "You're out on your feet."

"If I sit, I'll never get up again."

"What does it matter? They don't need you right now, do they? They know you have to sleep."

"I guess," Tanner muttered, collapsing in the chair closest to the couch.

Melaine waited for him to say something, but he simply stared at her, his eyes so dark that she couldn't see beneath the surface. She'd spent the night telling herself that this time he'd do more than take her hand. He hadn't even done that. She had no idea what was going on inside him.

"Tell me," she said, putting off the time when she would have to ask. "What kept you busy all night?"

His voice rasping, he told her about five hospital admissions, a lift that would need major repairs, sections of cross-country trail that couldn't be used for days. Three of the downhill runs had been closed to skiers, but that wouldn't last long and shouldn't cause a major inconvenience. He knew less about damage in the village itself, but then his concern had been with lives, not property.

"It could have been so much worse." Tanner pressed the back of his hand to his forehead. "When I think about that—"

"Then don't think. Every time I do it scares me."

"Does it? You weren't able to sleep?"

"What's sleep?" When he didn't answer, when he went on staring at her, Melaine continued. "You didn't go home. I thought you might."

"No . . . Amber? She's upstairs?"

"She passed out on the way out here." *Touch me. Why don't you touch me?* "Carol took care of her."

"Good." Tanner's head started to loll back. He straightened with a start. "Chris."

"Chris?" Melaine repeated. "What about him?"

"I called him yesterday. Told him Amber and you were missing."

"You did?" Melaine tried to imagine the conversation. Had Tanner said anything—anything that might make Chris think she'd been negligent. "What did he say?"

"I didn't give him much opportunity to talk." Tanner looked around, finally focusing on the wall clock. "Six A.M. If he chartered a plane, he should be here already."

"Did you tell him to come?"

For a moment Tanner didn't seem to comprehend her question. "Wouldn't you?" he asked finally. After looking at the clock again, he went back to staring at her. Melaine shifted slowly, stiffly, feeling the power of his scrutiny. Finally, grunting, Tanner pushed himself to his feet and walked over to the telephone. He dialed the operator and requested that she call a motel in Aspen for him. A minute later he asked to be connected with Chris Landa's room.

"Tanner," Melaine said. "What are you doing?"

"Trying to find Amber's father." The short sentence carried no warmth. Melaine tried to stand. She had to reach him before he said the wrong thing to Chris. Only, her ribs screamed a protest and she fell back, panting.

"Chris," Tanner said. "It's Tanner Harris. What the hell are you doing there? Yeah. I know what time it is. I asked you a question. Why aren't you here?"

Once again Melaine tried to push herself off the couch. The controlled energy in Tanner's voice chilled her blood. Anger she could handle. She almost expected that. But he sounded like a man who'd stepped into a boxing ring and didn't give a damn. He'd conquer or be conquered. The outcome didn't matter.

"Yeah. She's safe. I found her hours ago. Did you hear

that? Hours. If you gave a damn, you'd know that. No. I didn't try to reach you last night. Isn't that your job?"

Trembling, Melaine stretched out her hand. "Tanner!" she gasped. "Don't. Please!"

He turned toward her, but nothing in him softened. He pressed the receiver against his ear, his facial muscles knotted. He spoke through clenched teeth. "You figure it out, Chris. I can't live your life for you. No. She doesn't have anything to say to you." With that he hung up.

Melaine found her voice. "Tanner!" She wrapped her hand around her throat, heart pounding. "What did you do?"

"You heard."

"I heard you accuse Chris—"

"You heard me tell him he's a rotten father. He is, you know."

"No. Tanner, don't you know what you've done?"

"I know exactly what I've done. And it's about time he heard it. From me. You'll never tell him the truth."

"You?" Melaine repeated. "You? Tanner, you don't—"

"I know. I don't have a stake in this." Tanner towered over her. "I dropped everything I was supposed to do yesterday and went looking for you. For Amber. But I'm expected to stay in the background. To remain silent and civilized."

Melaine stared at the phone, then turned back toward Tanner.

"I can't do it." Tanner sounded exhausted as if the confrontation with her had stripped him of what little strength he had left. "I can't pretend last night didn't scare me like I've never been scared in my life. And I'm not sorry I said what I did."

"He'll come," Melaine managed. "He'll take Amber away."

"That's all you can think about? That he'll come for her? Damn it, he fell asleep not knowing whether she was safe. Alive."

Melaine couldn't listen. This time she managed to plant her feet under her and rock to her feet. She clutched her side, aware that Tanner hadn't said or done anything to lessen her pain. "You don't know. Maybe he couldn't get a flight—"

"Then why wasn't he burning up the phone lines? Damn it, Melaine. You want me to be civilized around a man who'll put anything before his daughter. He might have you jumping through his sick hoops, but I won't do it."

No. Of course he wouldn't. Tanner wasn't a man to back down. Only, he didn't have as much at stake. His life didn't revolve around the little girl sleeping upstairs. "He loves—"

"I don't think he's capable of the emotion. Look, I can't take back what I said, and I'm so tired I can't think straight. You aren't in any better shape."

Whether she was exhausted or not wasn't the issue. Still, he was right. Now wasn't the time to try to talk. "He—did he say what he was going to do?"

"I didn't give him the chance to give me his itinerary." Tanner ran his hand over his chin and frowned. "Call him if you think you have to. I won't be here to tell you what to say."

Trembling, Melaine watched as Tanner turned and walked out the door. She braced herself against the couch arm, listening to the sound of his truck pulling away. Had it only been a few minutes ago that that had been the most welcome sound in the world? When she could no longer hear anything, Melaine made her way over to the stairs and stared up toward the darkened bedrooms. Her body shivered with the need for sleep. Terrified that her time with Amber had come to an end, she tried to force herself to climb.

But her body refused to obey. Finally, groaning with something that had nothing to do with physical weakness, Melaine returned to the couch and lowered herself back onto it. She pulled the blanket around her shoulders, staring out the window as the morning sun brushed the horizon with a rose-tinted kiss. The last time she'd seen the sun, she'd prayed Tanner would find her before it was too late.

He'd found her.

And now it was too late.

For them. For everything.

"Tanner." Tears washed down her cheeks. She didn't bother trying to wipe them away. "Tanner."

FIFTEEN

Seven A.M. came and went. Amber didn't stir. Melaine had spent the hour since Tanner left trying to shut off her mind and heart so she could fall asleep. It didn't work. She couldn't stop the reverberation of the words that had and hadn't been said here.

Tanner had attacked Chris. In the past when she tried to convince Chris that she, not he, would make a better parent, he'd refused to listen. He'd talked about dedication and determination and family ties and told her she was free to leave.,

He'd been wrong. She hadn't been free to chart her own life since the first day she held Amber. For the sake of her self-esteem, she'd found it necessary to walk out of Chris's world, but she couldn't turn her back on Amber.

And now, oh, God, that decision had cost her Tanner.

At first when the phone rang, she could only stare at it. Carol? No. The pregnant woman needed her sleep. Tanner? Had he fallen into bed only to toss and turn, his thoughts as unhinged as hers? Would he call her back, ask that they try to find a way through this impasse?

No. Tanner had said they needed time.

"Melaine? Did I get you up?"

Melaine held on to the receiver and willed herself to

breathe. She stared out the window, trying to convince herself that the sun would go on rising. "Chris."

"Yeah. Chris. Did I wake you?"

"No. No. I've been—"

"It's a mess here," he interrupted. "I tried to tell Tanner that, but he wouldn't listen. I'm having a hell of a time finding a place to live. The rents are insane and there aren't any vacancies. I absolutely *have* to hire a foreman to run the manufacturing end of things. I've got three candidates to interview today."

"Oh." Melaine ran her hand over her side, vaguely aware of the layers of gauze. She wished the same padding was over her heart.

"One of them lives here. I could call him and cancel, but the other two are coming from out of state. They're due in in about an hour. I tried to explain that to Tanner but—I caught the news about your earthquake just before I went to bed. They said no one had been badly injured. I took it to mean that everyone was accounted for."

"Did you?"

"You understand, don't you? What, really, could I do if I dropped everything and flew to Mammoth? I'm not trained to help in rescue operations. I'd just be in the way. I decided to make sure I could be contacted at any time. That way, if either you or Tanner needed to get in touch with me, you wouldn't have any problems."

"Me?" As she'd done earlier with Tanner, Melaine clutched her throat. She felt out of control. For so long she'd gauged her every word with Chris, but she'd forgotten how. Her raw emotions ruled her. "Didn't Tanner tell you? I was with Amber. There was no way I could get to a telephone."

"Wait. Yes. He did tell me. I'm sorry. I guess, what with everything, I forgot."

He'd forgotten that she, too, had been caught by the avalanche? "I broke three ribs," she said, her tone stripped of all emotion. "I couldn't move. It was almost dark when they found me. Amber may have saved my life. Did you know that? No, of course you don't. She found Tanner and brought him to me."

Chris whistled. "She did that?"

"Did you hear me?" Melaine stressed. She wanted to close her eyes so she could concentrate fully, but she needed to see the sunrise. It was going to be a beautiful day—clear, cold. Maybe studying the sun would help her understand what was happening to her. "It happened so fast, tons of snow plunging toward us. All I had time to do was shove Amber out of the way. Otherwise—otherwise she might have been killed."

"Oh, my God."

"Chris?" She shouldn't say another word. But, driven by lack of sleep, pain, her fury at Chris, the sound of Tanner's truck pulling away, she was unable to be anything except honest. "Why didn't you call here last night?"

"Why? Have you ever tried to get through during an emergency? The lines are all clogged up—"

"Did you try?"

"No. That's what I—"

"Tanner told you that your daughter was missing, and yet you fell asleep? You relied on TV reports? You decided that interviewing people came before learning for yourself that your daughter was all right? Chris, we've been talking for five minutes, and you haven't asked to speak to Amber. Didn't it occur to you that she might need to hear your voice? Be held by her father?"

Melaine caught the sound of Chris breathing, but she didn't care. She stepped as close to the window as the telephone cord would allow. "I don't understand." Her voice sounded thin. Thin and yet incredibly strong. "I've never understood you. You say you love Amber. I think, in your own way, you do. But, Chris, if it was me and I'd heard that my child was lost, I would have been here even if it meant moving heaven and earth. I would have forgotten I had a business to run. It wouldn't occur to me that I was supposed to interview someone, or look for a house. Without my daughter, none of those other things would have mattered."

"She's my daughter, not yours."

In the past those words would have been enough to destroy Melaine, but not any longer. A dam inside her had burst. There was no stopping the flood of emotion. "Then, damn it, why don't you act like a father? Chris. She deserves better."

"Better?"

"She deserves someone who risks getting killed herself because a child's life means more than her own." Feeling hot, feeling cold, Melaine swayed under the impact of what she'd just said. "If you loved her, the way a child deserves to be loved, you'd be here now."

Melaine counted the seconds, ticking them off. She'd spent years clutching those just-released emotions to her, feeling them grow and swirl, wrenching them back into their prison when they threatened to break free. Now they'd exploded from her; in the end, there'd really been only one thing to say. *If you love her, you'd be here.*

Tanner, by showing her the way, had made the difference. He'd unlocked the prison gates and forced her to be utterly, cruelly honest.

"She—you—you're both all right?"

"She's sleeping."

"Then let her sleep. I'll talk to her later. Melaine? What you just said. You mean it, don't you? That's not just anger talking."

He sounded old. Tired. "I'm not angry, Chris. It's so much more than that."

"Yeah. It is. You saved her life?"

"Maybe. I don't know."

"But that's what you were thinking when it happened. That her life came first."

"Chris, I don't know if I was thinking. I acted out of instinct."

"Instinct." The word trailed off as if Chris had never used or heard it before. "You've got quite a hook, Melaine. You and Tanner."

"What are you talking about?" She'd been ready to have Chris hang up on her. She hadn't cared; she'd deal with the consequences of—finally—total honesty later. But this old-sounding man had her off balance.

"I'm talking about people shooting from the hip. Melaine? Let me talk, will you? I'm thinking of something. The way I was raised."

"What—"

"What does this have to do with today? Maybe everything. You know my parents. The way they are. I shake my father's hand because that's what he expects. I kiss my mother on the cheek because that's what she wants. We don't hug. We don't call each other just to talk. They never ask how Amber's doing."

"Oh, Chris." Melaine perched on the edge of the couch, her head pounding. She knew those things. She'd just never been able to get Chris to talk about them.

"I want her to have more than I got."

Melaine closed her eyes and concentrated on getting air into her lungs.

"Will you take her? Give her what I can't?"

When Amber came downstairs, Melaine offered to fix her breakfast. Amber had a better idea. What if Melaine sat on the kitchen stool while Amber cooked pancakes. Although Amber overfilled the measuring cup, Melaine watched in silence. *Raise her. Give her what I can't.*

She knew she should tell Amber about the conversation, but the words were too new with her. She was going to be Amber's mother, not just in her heart as she'd always been, but to the world as well.

To Tanner.

She had to tell him.

Maybe it didn't matter to him, she thought as Amber set orange juice in front of her. They hadn't said much last night or this morning, and what they had, carried no promise of a future. Tanner had accused Chris of not putting his daughter first in his life. Terrified that he'd destroyed everything between her and Amber, Melaine had tried to make him listen. He hadn't been interested. Chris needed to face the truth. That was all Tanner understood, or wanted to understand.

In the end, Tanner had turned out to be right.

But even with Chris's words lending song to her heart, Melaine knew that nothing had changed between her and Tanner.

"How would you like to go see Carol and Bert a little later?" Melaine asked. "You could thank them for everything they did."

"Aren't you coming?"

"I'll take you there, but I need to talk to Tanner."

Amber's face fell. "Can't I go? I want to thank him, too."

"You can do that a little later," Melaine promised. "Tanner and I need to talk some grown-up stuff."

"Good or bad grown-up stuff?"

Melaine tried to smile, but she knew she'd failed. Bad? Good? That depended on whether Tanner wanted anything to do with her. He'd never said "I love you." She'd never looked deeply enough inside herself to know, really know, what she felt for him.

It wasn't enough simply to be lovers. It wasn't enough that he'd spent hours looking for her. That, after all, had been his job. But love—

Loving a woman who would be raising another man's child.

Who maybe didn't know the meaning of the words when it came to a man.

Once she'd forced down what she could of her breakfast, Melaine called Carol. "I have to run an errand," she said vaguely. "I don't know how long I'll be gone."

"I have a pretty good idea what your errand is. Otherwise you wouldn't be forcing your battered body out of the house. By the way, when Bert went to work he noticed that *his* truck is at his place."

"Thank you."

"You're welcome. The reason why Tanner isn't with you, is it insurmountable?"

"I don't know. Maybe."

"I'm sorry. Look, leave her as long as you need to."

Melaine asked Amber to go upstairs and pick something for both of them to wear. She made her way into the downstairs bathroom, where she brushed her teeth, washed her face, and raked a comb through her hair. Just the idea of taking a shower exhausted her. By the time she'd forced her aching body into the loose slacks and blouse Amber had chosen, she wasn't sure she could make it outside. Amber helped by putting on her boots and holding her coat while she inched into it.

"I'm never going to hurt my ribs," Amber declared. "I'm never going to break anything."

"I hope you don't." Melaine gave her a brave if brief smile. "It isn't much fun."

By holding on to Amber's shoulder, Melaine managed to make it down the outside stairs. She gripped the car keys, wondering how in the world she'd force her reluctant body behind the wheel. At least dealing with her injuries didn't leave enough of her mind free to concentrate on what she'd tell Tanner, or what he'd say to her.

She'd opened the door of the Jeep and taken a deep breath when she heard the sound. Tanner had returned.

Leaning against the vehicle, Melaine waited. He seemed to take a long time getting out of his truck. When he finally emerged, she saw that he was carrying a small paper bag. Ignoring her, Tanner walked over to Amber. "You're up already? I thought you'd sleep all day."

"No. I like mornings. Did you get any sleep?"

"A little," Tanner said, and Melaine knew he'd lied. "Where are you going?"

Amber told him. Tanner nodded but said nothing. Instead, making a ceremony of it, he handed Amber his package. "Something I thought you might need. You—you can open it later if you want."

By then Amber had already unwrapped the bag. She reached in and pulled out a pair of bright-red gloves with the size tag still on them. Tanner cleared his throat. "They might be too small, but you lost yours when . . . Why don't you try them on."

Grinning, Amber shoved her fingers into a glove. "Perfect." She turned toward Melaine, her hand uplifted. "They're all red. Just like the other ones." She whirled back around to face Tanner. "How did you know my size?"

For the first time since he'd pulled up, Tanner glanced Melaine's way. The look lasted a half second, not long enough for her to see anything except the dark in his eyes. "I, ah, remembered how your hand felt in mine. That helped. Why—why don't you—"

Suddenly Tanner pulled Amber to him. In the crisp, silent morning air, Melaine heard him breathing. The sound was ragged, that of a man trying not to cry. As emotion washed over her, Tanner took another raw breath.

Forgetting everything except what was being revealed to her, she stepped closer. Tanner stood with his arms around Amber and his face buried in the girl's hair. Melaine saw him shudder.

A moment later, Tanner gently pushed Amber away. His eyes on the girl he again cleared his throat. "I've been telling everyone about you. About how brave you were."

"I wasn't really. I was scared."

Tanner touched his fingers to Amber's cheek. "We were all pretty scared last night. Look, I . . . why don't you find scissors so you can cut off the tag. Then you can try on the other one."

Nodding, Amber wrapped her arms around Tanner's waist. "I forgot all about losing my gloves. How did you remember?"

"How? When I was trying to fall asleep, I thought about when I saw you climbing over the snow. I remembered how cold your hands were."

"You held them. You blew on them and rubbed them and they weren't cold anymore."

"Yes. I guess I did." Tanner leaned forward and planted a kiss on the top of Amber's head. "I'm—glad I could find red. I like the color on you."

"Me, too," Amber said, and turned her face upward. This time Tanner kissed her on the forehead, holding her gently in place. Amber giggled, then squeezed Tanner back.

A minute later, she turned and bounded up the stairs, the gloves clutched against her middle. "Don't go away," she called. "I'm going to see if they're the same color red as my ski outfit."

Tanner stared after her, his body not quite shuddering, not quite still.

Shaken with an emotion of her own, Melaine tried to close a little of the distance separating them. She couldn't make herself move. "You feel it, don't you?"

"It?"

"What Amber has done to my heart."

Although Tanner stared at her without blinking, Melaine didn't drop her eyes. He'd shaved, but that had done little to wipe the exhaustion from him. He looked so distant, so unapproachable. "I didn't know. Until I saw her last night and let myself think about what might have happened, I didn't know."

"I hope you do now. Because—"

"Because why?"

She couldn't say the words. He deserved to know that

she'd be raising Amber, and yet she put it off. He hadn't touched her; she hadn't touched him.

He'd never told her he loved her.

Neither had she.

"I thought you'd be asleep," she said instead.

"I couldn't. Where were you going?"

To see you. To expose myself in a way I've never been exposed before. "Carol's. Amber wanted to see her."

"What?" Tanner looked incredulous. "You've got three broken ribs and yet you're going to climb in a car and go to a woman who's perfectly capable of driving out here? I don't buy that."

"What are you doing here?" Melaine sidestepped his question. "I thought you said we needed time to think."

"We did. That's over."

She didn't follow his train of thought, or if she did, she wasn't sure she wanted to. "If you're going to start your argument about Amber all over again, I won't listen. I don't have to."

"What are you talking about?"

"About not having to give Amber up. I talked to Chris this morning. He's going to let me raise her."

Tanner looked as if she'd punched him in the gut. She longed to tell him that the miracle wouldn't have happened if he hadn't made Chris face facts, if he hadn't rubbed her so raw that she'd been incapable of anything except speaking the truth. But she couldn't say a word.

"Talked. What happened?"

She told him, keeping the telling brief, sliding over much of it so she wouldn't start to cry. "I still can't believe it," she finished. "After all these years . . . He isn't a bad man. It isn't his fault."

"No. I don't suppose it is. So, Melaine, what happens now?"

"Now? Now I become Amber's mother."

"No." He shook his head. "That's not what I'm talking about. What happens with us?"

Nothing. I'd never try to tie you to this. "Didn't you hear me? I'm going to be raising another man's child."

"I heard you. By yourself. That's what you're saying, isn't it?"

Yes. Because I have no choice. "Tanner?" She faltered and tried again. "You and I, we've been through a lot together. I'll never try to deny that. But physical attraction, that isn't enough."

"Isn't it?" Tanner ran a hand through his hair, looking for all the world like a man out on his feet.

"I think you know the answer to that." Melaine took a backward step. She understood nothing of Tanner's thoughts. She understood even less of her own. "Tanner, I'm going to try to get my life together. Give Amber the security she needs. That's all I can think about."

"No."

"No what?"

"Amber isn't all you have to think about. The only thing I know is that I'm part of your life, or I would be if you let me."

"Let?" The hurricane of emotion she'd felt while she was talking to Chris washed through her again. "Amber, she isn't anything to you. She's everything to me."

"She isn't anything to me?" Tanner glanced up at the house. "You don't get it, do you? Either that or you won't let yourself see it. I happen to love that little girl. No. Don't," he said when she opened her mouth. "Let me finish. The other day I told you I wouldn't let myself fall in love with her. As if I had a choice. Finding her out in the snow taught me how little control I have over certain emotions."

Melaine concentrated on breathing. It didn't help. "You love her?"

"Hook, line, and sinker. Is that so hard to understand?"

"I—don't know."

He reached out for her, but she shied away. If he

touched her, she might shatter into a thousand pieces like hand-spun glass.

"Melaine. Tell me what you're thinking."

That I've never been this way before. "I wish you'd never come to care for her," she whispered.

"What? I don't believe you."

"Don't you?" Melaine asked. She felt as if her world had been turned on its axis. She was tipping crazily, trying to right herself. If only she could turn and run. Yet, she wanted to stay. "It isn't fair for you. Feeling the way you do about her. Feeling the way you do about me."

"What do I feel about you?"

Melaine closed her eyes. That way she didn't have to look at the morning sun, or at Tanner. "You don't love me."

"I don't what?"

"Love me," she repeated.

He grabbed her arms. She kept her eyes closed, swaying, barely aware of the pain in her side. She remembered the feel of her sisters as they pressed against her in the police station. And she remembered something else, that when her mother finally came back, she hadn't kissed any of her children.

The memories faded away, and there was only Tanner.

"What makes you think I don't love you?" he asked.

Did he really expect an answer? Melaine spoke through a fog, not caring what he said. "You've never told me."

"I never, oh, my God. Melaine, look at me."

She obeyed. Expecting to find fury or worse, pity, his compassion almost undermined her. "Are you listening?" he asked. When she nodded, he went on. "What I felt, what I feel for you . . . I've never experienced that before. It's powerful, overwelming, like what hit me when I found Amber last night, only different. Complicated by other emotions. The first time we met, hunger took over. I'd never felt that way before. I didn't know how to handle it. Then, when I saw you here, that hunger happened again. Only, it was more than that. I was falling in love, falling in a way I didn't know was possible. Only, you didn't say anything. Not once did you tell me how you felt."

Couldn't he tell? Her every nerve ending had been alive with the emotion. "I couldn't."

"Why not?"

"I didn't know how. I didn't dare."

"Melaine," Tanner pressed. "What are you talking about?"

Years ago a child had put her life in a woman's hands. Only, trust had been shattered. That child had grown into a woman who'd married a man incapable of giving her what she needed.

She'd learned her lesson. Don't trust. Don't be vulnerable. Don't fall in love.

Only, she had no more control over what she felt for Tanner than what she felt for Amber. And trying to keep that from him, and herself, trying to protect her hungry and defenseless heart, had nearly cost her everything.

"I'm afraid. I was afraid."

"Of what?"

"Of being vulnerable again. My mother, Chris—"

"Oh, God."

Through tear-misted eyes, Melaine read Tanner's emotion. She swayed, but he held her against him. Held her strong and safe and sure. He hadn't tried to hide from her what he felt for Amber. Hadn't he just exposed his emotions in all their raw honesty? A man who could do that, who could feel like that for a child, was capable of other kinds of love.

The kind of love she needed.

The kind she wanted to give in return.

"I'm sorry," she whispered and folded herself into him. "I wanted . . . So many times I wanted to tell you."

"What? What did you want to tell me?"

She blinked. When her vision cleared, Melaine saw that

Tanner was smiling. He was waiting for her, patient, understanding, forgiving.

"That I love you."

"Enough to marry me? To be part of a family?"

The cabin door opened and closed with a squeak. Still, Melaine didn't take her eyes off Tanner. "A family," she whispered.

"A family," he repeated.

SHARE THE FUN ...
SHARE YOUR NEW-FOUND TREASURE!!

You don't want to let your new books out of your sight? That's okay. Your friends can get their own. Order below.

No. 25 LOVE WITH INTEREST by Darcy Rice
Stephanie & Elliot find $47,000,000 *plus* interest—true love!

No. 26 NEVER A BRIDE by Leanne Banks
The last thing Cassie wanted was a relationship. Joshua had other ideas.

No. 27 GOLDILOCKS by Judy Christenberry
David and Susan join forces and get tangled in their own web.

No. 28 SEASON OF THE HEART by Ann Hammond
Can Lane and Maggie's newfound feelings stand the test of time?

No. 29 FOSTER LOVE by Janis Reams Hudson
Morgan comes home to claim his children but Sarah claims his heart.

No. 30 REMEMBER THE NIGHT by Sally Falcon
Joanna throws caution to the wind. Is Nathan fantasy or reality?

No. 31 WINGS OF LOVE by Linda Windsor
Mac & Kelly soar to heights of ecstasy. Will they have a smooth landing?

No. 32 SWEET LAND OF LIBERTY by Ellen Kelly
Brock has a secret and Liberty's freedom could be in serious jeopardy!

No. 33 A TOUCH OF LOVE by Patricia Hagan
Kelly seeks peace and quiet and finds paradise in Mike's arms.

No. 34 NO EASY TASK by Chloe Summers
Hunter is wary when Doone delivers a package that will change his life.

No. 35 DIAMOND ON ICE by Lacey Dancer
Diana could melt even the coldest of hearts. Jason hasn't a chance.

No. 36 DADDY'S GIRL by Janice Kaiser
Slade wants more than Andrea is willing to give. Who wins?

No. 37 ROSES by Caitlin Randall
It's an inside job & K.C. helps Brett find more than the thief!

No. 38 HEARTS COLLIDE by Ann Patrick
Matthew finds big trouble and it's spelled P-a-u-l-a.

No. 39 QUINN'S INHERITANCE by Judi Lind
Gabe and Quinn share an inheritance and find an even greater fortune.

No. 40 CATCH A RISING STAR by Laura Phillips
Justin is seeking fame; Beth shows him an even greater reward.

No. 41 SPIDER'S WEB by Allie Jordan
Silvia's quiet life explodes when Fletcher shows up on her doorstep.

No. 42 TRUE COLORS by Dixie DuBois
Julian helps Nikki find herself again but will she have room for him?

No. 43 DUET by Patricia Collinge
Two parts of a puzzle, Adam & Marina glue their lives together with love.

No. 44 DEADLY COINCIDENCE by Denise Richards
J.D.'s instincts tell him he's not wrong; Laurie's heart says trust him.

No. 45 PERSONAL BEST by Margaret Watson
Tess knows she must avoid Nick at all costs—even if he is the most attractive man she'd ever met!

No. 46 ONE ON ONE by JoAnn Barbour
Loie doesn't trust Vincent—he's handsome, sexy and full of the devil; if that's not enough—he's now her student!!

No. 47 STERLING'S REASONS by Joey Light
Joe tries desperately to run from life and his memories. Sterling won't allow it.

No. 48 SNOW SOUNDS by Heather Williams
Tanner couldn't believe Melaine was back in his life and on his mountain. In the quiet of their mountain, they find each other again.

Kismet Romances
Dept. 691, P. O. Box 41820, Philadelphia, PA 19101-9828

Please send the books I've indicated below. Check or money order only—no cash, stamps or C.O.D.s (PA residents, add 6% sales tax). I am enclosing $2.95 plus 75¢ handling fee for *each* book ordered.

Total Amount Enclosed: $_____.

___ No. 25	___ No. 31	___ No. 37	___ No. 43
___ No. 26	___ No. 32	___ No. 38	___ No. 44
___ No. 27	___ No. 33	___ No. 39	___ No. 45
___ No. 28	___ No. 34	___ No. 40	___ No. 46
___ No. 29	___ No. 35	___ No. 41	___ No. 47
___ No. 30	___ No. 36	___ No. 42	___ No. 48

Please Print:
Name _____
Address _____ Apt. No. _____
City/State _____ Zip _____

Allow four to six weeks for delivery. Quantities limited.